NOT MY DAUGHTER

EVA RAE THOMAS MYSTERY - BOOK 16

WILLOW ROSE

What's coming next from Willow Rose?

Join Willow Rose's VIP Newsletter to get exclusive updates about New Releases, Giveaways, and FREE ebooks.

Just scan this QR code with your phone and click on the link:

Books by the Author

HARRY HUNTER MYSTERY SERIES

- All The Good Girls
- Run Girl Run
- No Other Way
- Never Walk Alone

MARY MILLS MYSTERY SERIES

- What Hurts the Most
- You Can Run
- You Can't Hide
- Careful Little Eyes

EVA RAE THOMAS MYSTERY SERIES

- So We Lie
- Don't Lie to me
- What you did
- Never Ever
- Say You Love me
- Let Me Go
- It's Not Over
- Not Dead yet
- To Die For
- Such A Good Girl
- Little Did She Know
- You Better Run
- Say It Isn't So
- Too Pretty To Die
- Till Death Do Us Part
- Rest In Peace
- Dark Little Secrets
- Not My Daughter

EMMA FROST SERIES

- ITSY BITSY SPIDER
- MISS DOLLY HAD A DOLLY
- RUN, RUN AS FAST AS YOU CAN
- CROSS YOUR HEART AND HOPE TO DIE
- PEEK-A-BOO I SEE YOU
- TWEEDLEDUM AND TWEEDLEDEE
- EASY AS ONE, TWO, THREE
- THERE'S NO PLACE LIKE HOME
- SLENDERMAN
- WHERE THE WILD ROSES GROW
- WALTZING MATHILDA
- DRIP DROP DEAD
- BLACK FROST

JACK RYDER SERIES

- HIT THE ROAD JACK
- SLIP OUT THE BACK JACK
- THE HOUSE THAT JACK BUILT
- BLACK JACK
- GIRL NEXT DOOR
- HER FINAL WORD
- DON'T TELL

REBEKKA FRANCK SERIES

- ONE, TWO…HE IS COMING FOR YOU
- THREE, FOUR…BETTER LOCK YOUR DOOR
- FIVE, SIX…GRAB YOUR CRUCIFIX
- SEVEN, EIGHT…GONNA STAY UP LATE
- NINE, TEN…NEVER SLEEP AGAIN
- ELEVEN, TWELVE…DIG AND DELVE
- THIRTEEN, FOURTEEN…LITTLE BOY UNSEEN
- BETTER NOT CRY
- TEN LITTLE GIRLS
- IT ENDS HERE

MYSTERY/THRILLER/HORROR NOVELS

- Sorry Can't Save You
- In One Fell Swoop
- Umbrella Man
- Blackbird Fly
- To Hell in a Handbasket
- Edwina

HORROR SHORT-STORIES

- Mommy Dearest
- The Bird
- Better watch out
- Eenie, Meenie
- Rock-a-Bye Baby
- Nibble, Nibble, Crunch
- Humpty Dumpty
- Chain Letter

PARANORMAL SUSPENSE/ROMANCE NOVELS

- In Cold Blood
- The Surge
- Girl Divided

THE VAMPIRES OF SHADOW HILLS SERIES

- FLESH AND BLOOD
- BLOOD AND FIRE
- FIRE AND BEAUTY
- BEAUTY AND BEASTS
- BEASTS AND MAGIC
- MAGIC AND WITCHCRAFT
- WITCHCRAFT AND WAR
- WAR AND ORDER
- ORDER AND CHAOS
- CHAOS AND COURAGE

THE AFTERLIFE SERIES

- BEYOND
- SERENITY
- ENDURANCE
- COURAGEOUS

THE WOLFBOY CHRONICLES

- A GYPSY SONG
- I AM WOLF

DAUGHTERS OF THE JAGUAR

- SAVAGE
- BROKEN

Prologue
PARADISE KEY, THURSDAY EVENING

THE SHADOWS COVERED the beach like a dark blanket. Hidden in the rustling palm leaves was a dark figure. The figure stayed crouched, muscles tense, breathing slowly and quietly while watching through the leaves, eyes focused intently on the two people walking under the bright moonlight.

"I really love this place," one of them said, their voice carried on a warm, salty breeze. The tone was cheerful, mixed with a light laugh that stood out against the humid, charged night air.

"It's so quiet here, and no one can see us," came the reply in a deep, smooth voice that blended seamlessly with the gentle sound of the waves crashing against the shore.

The couple strolled along the moonlit beach, completely absorbed in their private universe. Their hands were entwined in a tight grip that spoke of silent promises and unspoken secrets. Bathed in the glow from the moon, their outlines shimmered on the cool, powdery sand, each step etching a temporary story quickly swallowed by the advancing tide. The gentle scent of salt mingled with the crisp night air, carrying memories of distant summers and long-forgotten dreams.

"Look at the moon," one whispered, their voice as soft and

elusive as the frothy edges of the breakers caressing the shore. "It almost seems to be smiling at us."

"Maybe it really is," the other replied, their tone laced with wonder, as though the night itself celebrated their joy.

Hidden behind a cluster of gracefully swaying palms, the Observer watched intently. Every rustle of the fronds and each glimmer of moonlight dancing on the undulating water seemed to feed into the Observer's growing bitterness. With eyes that shimmered like fractured glass, the Observer took in every detail—the way their laughter mingled with the night's sounds, each tender word forming part of a tapestry that deepened the cracks in the Observer's own fractured soul.

"Race you to the pier!" one of the lovers suddenly exclaimed, prompting an energetic burst that transformed playful banter into a jubilant sprint. Bare feet pounded the sandy stretch, leaving behind hurried, fleeting imprints that whispered of mischief and vibrant excitement.

"Hey, no fair!" came the delighted protest, playful yet tinged with a challenge that harmonized effortlessly with the rhythmic lull of the crashing surf and the soft serenade of the night.

In the deep shadows, the Observer tensed as if the palm trees themselves were murmuring clandestine secrets just for them. The vast, star-scattered sky and trembling, murmuring waves bore silent testimony to the couple's tender exchange. Each happy word echoed like a bittersweet reminder of the Observer's own isolation. When a teasing "Wait up!" floated through the humid night, it was instantly met by a burst of genuine laughter—laughter that stirred up old memories and unexpected emotions, sharpening the sting of the Observer's discontent.

In the cool, shadowed confines of that secluded part of the beach, the Observer's inner monologue churned with dark, raw feelings. Every chuckle and every loving whisper exchanged between the couple intensified an overwhelming sense of betrayal and loss. It was as if the beauty of the night was marred by an undercurrent of bitterness that the Observer could not dispel.

"The night sky is as beautiful as your eyes," one murmured

softly, their words lingering in the heavy, humid air like the delicate trace of a perfumed handkerchief.

"Careful, or you'll start sounding like a poet," the other joked, nudging them playfully with a touch that recalled a history rich with shared smiles and quiet moments.

"Would that be so terrible?" came the lighthearted retort. "I think poets have their own charm."

"Only if your verses are as terrible as your puns," replied the other quickly, punctuating the exchange with a soft laugh and a smile that encapsulated years of shared secrets. It was a moment so delicate that even the Observer's clenched hand, gripping the rough, weathered bark of a nearby palm, tightened in silent, desperate anger.

Unperturbed by the invisible gaze, the couple resumed their slow, rhythmic walk along the shore, entirely unaware of the hidden eyes that followed each graceful step. Their muted contentment painted a scene of tranquil intimacy—a stark contrast to the Observer's turbulent mix of envy and simmering resentment. Every soft giggle and murmured endearment from the lovers was recorded in intricate detail in the Observer's mind, each stoking the flames of a dark, vengeful plan.

"How cute," the Observer thought bitterly, dismissing every spark of uncomplicated affection that filled the humid night. Deep within, a silent scheme began to take shape—dangerous and insidious, much like the shadows that cloaked the beach. Every sliver of laughter and carefree whisper was etched into the Observer's memory, fueling a pledge of retribution that thrummed in time with an increasingly erratic heartbeat.

The laughter that might once have been a balm now sliced through the Observer's heart. "Stop it, please. Just stop," came a barely audible plea, as though the night itself could silence the chaos inside. Then, suddenly, there was an intimate moment—a slow, deliberate kiss that carved into the Observer's core with its electrifying closeness. As their lips met, it was as if unseen fingers stirred the sand beneath, with each grain silently bearing witness to their intimate communion.

After the kiss broke, soft, secretive words filled the humid air—a language shared only by these two souls. They turned back to their path, their retreat accompanied by the gentle shifting of sand and the soothing crash of the waves. "Look at it," one murmured, extending an arm toward the horizon where the sea kissed the sky under a subtle, silver glow.

"Beautiful," the other agreed, squeezing the extended hand in a quiet gesture meant to capture and hold that perfect moment in time.

Meanwhile, hidden among the whispering palms, the Observer's breath came in short, ragged bursts. The sincere, joyful laughter and the tender words, so freely given, cut deeply against a backdrop of turbulent, primitive emotions—a raw mix of bitterness, anger, and longing that no serene scene could ever dispel. Every tender gesture and playful movement was a stark reminder of a life the Observer once knew—a world that now lay just beyond reach.

With each heartbeat, the desire to step out of the shroud of darkness and reclaim what was lost grew insidiously stronger. The irregular pounding of the Observer's heart clashed with the soothing cadence of the night, trapping them in a prison of silent regret and unresolved grief. Yet even as the couple danced away into the distance, the promise of retribution promised a slow, deliberate release of long-held fury.

"Patience," the Observer muttered under their breath, as if to cool the smoldering intensity of their dark thoughts, "There's time." Gradually, the couple's laughter and affectionate voices receded, fading into the endless murmur of the tides. With every passing moment, the Observer's isolation deepened, while the vivid picture of the couple's bliss slowly dissolved into the boundless darkness.

As the lovers moved farther down the beach, their forms were occasionally illuminated by stray moonbeams filtering through scattered clouds. Their footprints—once vibrant symbols of their shared joy—vanished beneath the steady, unyielding tide. Deep within the Observer's mind, schematics of revenge began to twist and coil like serpents on a stormy night. Every playful glance and carefree laugh contributed another staccato note to a quiet crescendo that promised retribution.

"Let them laugh," the Observer whispered coldly, watching the figures gradually diminish until they were barely visible against the relentless surge of the surf. The couple's laughter dwindled to soft murmurs, their shadows stretching languidly along the cooling sand —a living testament to tender intimacy under the moon's silver glow. In the end, they melted into the horizon, becoming one with the deep, mysterious blues and purples of the nocturnal sky.

"Foolish children," the Observer thought silently, each word loaded with a resonance of old anger. The darkness thickened, blurring the couple's outline until only a faint echo of their presence remained.

"Let the dance begin," the Observer whispered in a low, dangerous tone—a promise that was both chilling and inevitable.

"Ready or not," they added calmly as they receded further into the shadows, "here I come."

Chapter 1
PARADISE KEY, FRIDAY AFTERNOON

THE BOAT'S deck swayed gently beneath me, a soothing motion that seemed to match the rhythm of my body. The endless expanse of turquoise water stretched before me, shimmering in the sun's warm rays. A gust of salty air brushed against my skin, carrying with it a sense of freedom and rejuvenation.

I settled into an empty seat, warmed by the sun, and pulled out a small notebook from my bag. It felt out of place in the middle of such vastness, but I opened it anyway, pen poised above the blank page.

"Hello, my new best friend," I whispered to the notebook, smiling as memories and thoughts flooded my mind.

I had recently taken up journaling upon a good friend's advice. I had been stressed—too stressed for months, and I could feel it in my body. It was time for something new.

"Try journaling," my friend Melissa said. "It has helped me a lot to generate structure of my thoughts when I'm stressed out."

I thought, why not? Give it a try.

And now that I was finally having some much-needed time away from my hectic life as a mom and FBI agent, I was going to reconnect with my old friends from Washington and their children on a private island in the Keys for the weekend. It was one of my friend's son—Mark's—twentieth birthday, and as usual, his mother would celebrate with an extravagant party for us all. This year, she had invited everyone to their private island where they usually vacationed every summer.

The pen glided across the page, my handwriting flowing like waves:

'Find myself again. Breathe. Let go of FBI agent Eva Rae and embrace being just me.'

I paused, gazing out at the peaceful ocean. Memories of conversations and moments shared with old friends danced at the edges of my mind—those moments of pure understanding and belonging.

"Six years..." I murmured to the horizon.

It had been six years since life's current carried me away from Washington to Florida's embrace. And now, here I stood on the brink of reconnecting with those bonds. Anticipation fluttered within me, eager to soar as I prepared to rekindle old friendships.

Memories swirled in my head, drawing me into a warm eddy of the past. The yearly zoo trip—our laughter echoing through the aviary, children's faces alight with wonder at the kaleidoscope of birds in flight. Olivia, her small hand in mine, as we trailed behind the group.

"Look, Mommy!" Her voice rose above the din, pointing to a peacock fanning its jeweled tail.

"Beautiful, just like you," I'd said, squeezing her hand.

Those days were spun from gold, and we mothers were a tapestry of shared experiences, with our kids as the threads binding us tightly.

Guilt gnawed at me sometimes, uprooting Olivia from that rich garden of friendships. But life's winds don't ask before they blow you across the map. Florida's sun promised new blooms, even if nostalgia occasionally watered the flowers of yesteryear. I had never regretted moving back home. It was the right thing to do at the time.

A vibration in my pocket jolted me back to the present. I fished out my phone, thumb-swiping the screen to life. Olivia's name lit up the display.

"Can't wait to see you, Mom! The island is amazing!!" her text read, punctuated by a rainbow of emojis.

My heart did a little pirouette. "Me too, sweetheart," I whispered, thumbs tapping out a reply.

She was already there and had been hanging out with her old friends for two days, having the time of her life.

"Prepare for hugs. Lots of them," I typed, sealing the message with a heart and hitting send.

The boat cut through the waves, carrying me closer to my girl, to shared histories, and to a weekend where Agent Thomas could hang up her badge and just be Eva Rae.

Chapter 2

THE NOTEBOOK'S crisp pages fluttered under my fingers as I scrawled the last few thoughts, a lump forming in my throat. Olivia had filled every corner of my heart with pride over these six years since we had last been with this group of people, her old friends. She'd blossomed from a shy teenager into a woman who faced her college classes and life with unwavering determination. She had come out as gay to everyone in her family and her friends and had dated a girl for some time, but it was over now.

The boat sliced through the water, a sleek predator heading for its lair. The island materialized from a blur on the horizon to an expanse of vivid greenery and ivory sands that stretched out like welcoming arms. I leaned over the railing, ocean spray kissing my cheeks as if beckoning me into the embrace of Paradise Key Private Resort.

"Almost there," I murmured, watching palm trees sway in a rhythm only nature could choreograph. The island's pristine beaches glistened under the sun, a canvas of untouched beauty I'd soon tread upon. My heart swelled, anticipation curling in my stomach like the gentle waves lapping at the boat's hull.

"Welcome to The Island," the captain announced as we approached the dock; his voice, a smooth baritone, seemed part of the breeze itself.

I stood, the boat steadying beneath me as if sharing my eagerness. Gathering my bag—a soft leather tote I'd chosen for both practicality and style—I slung it over my shoulder, feeling the weight of its contents: sunscreen, a novel I'd been meaning to finish, and the dresses. Oh, those dresses. A smile tugged at my lips, imagining the coming evenings, cosmos in hand, laughter mingling with the whisper of silk and chiffon against sun-kissed skin.

Stepping onto the pier, my sandals clicked against the weathered wood, each step a declaration of arrival. The opulence of the resort was almost jarring compared to my usual surroundings of sterile offices and crime scenes. Here, luxury awaited—no crime scene tape in sight.

"Time to swap FBI badges for bikinis," I joked to myself, my voice a low murmur drowned out by the rhythmic thud of my heart. The thought of lounging by the pool, wine glass perched nearby, felt like a fantasy about to unfold in vivid color. I couldn't wait to see my old friends. It was going to be a blast.

I paused, allowing myself a moment to scan the island. Every detail called out to be savored—the way the fronds cast dancing shadows on the ground, the scent of salt and blooming flowers weaving through the air, the infinity pool's crystal-clear waters mirroring the sky.

"Mrs. Thomas?" A gentle voice lilted from behind, belonging to one of the resort staff. He was a tall, sun-kissed young man with a friendly smile and eyes the color of the turquoise sea. He wore a crisp white shirt and khaki shorts, embodying the effortless charm of the island.

"Please, call me Eva," I corrected, offering him a nod of gratitude as he took my bag with practiced grace.

"Of course, Eva. Welcome to Paradise Key." His words were accompanied by the soft rustling of palm leaves swaying in the warm breeze. The air was fragrant with the scent of hibiscus and salt, and the gentle lapping of waves against the pristine sandy shore provided a soothing background melody. Lush greenery surrounded us, the vibrant colors of tropical flowers punctuating the landscape, making it feel like a slice of paradise nestled in the heart of the ocean.

"Thank you," I said, eyes still roaming the landscape. My mind wandered to lavish dinners under the stars, old friends, and the promise of memories yet to be made.

"Right this way," he gestured toward the main house, his uniform crisp against the casual backdrop.

"Lead on," I replied, stepping off the pier with a renewed sense of purpose. The weekend was about to begin, and I was ready for whatever it might bring.

My stride quickened as the main house came into view, each step a beat in the rhythm of anticipation.

"Can't wait to see how everyone's changed," I murmured to myself, my flip-flops scuffing against the stone pathway. "And to catch up on what everyone's been up to."

Ahead, the grandeur of the main house loomed, a testament to the kind of extravagance that punctuated the lives of my old friends. And yet, despite the luxury, there was an ease to the island—a whisper of serenity that even the opulence couldn't overshadow.

"Almost there," I breathed out, the muscles in my shoulders relaxing unconsciously. Olivia's latest text flashed in my mind—her excitement, her growth. Pride swelled within me, offering strength that grounded my nerves.

I halted just shy of the main entrance, caught by the sun's descent casting a golden hue over the lush landscape. I closed my eyes, the warmth on my skin a gentle reminder of life's fleeting beauty.

"Here's to new beginnings... and cherished pasts," I whispered, the weight of my investigative work, motherhood, and ever-evolving self momentarily lifted by the promise of a tranquil interlude. A deep breath filled my lungs, the perfumed air mingling with the resolve to soak in every second of serenity.

"Ready or not," I said to no one.

With a final, grounding breath, I stepped forward, ready to weave the weekend's tapestry of stories and secrets.

The laughter and rhythmic beat of music spilled out from the main house's open windows, wrapping around me like a warm embrace as I approached.

I paused, a smile breaking across my face; these were the women who had been part of my life for years, their laughter the same as it had echoed back in Washington.

"Finally!" A voice cut through the symphony of merriment, and the silhouette framed by the doorway materialized into Kara's welcoming figure.

"Kara!" I replied, matching her enthusiasm as I closed the distance between us.

"Look at you, Eva Rae! Florida sun suits you," she beamed, pulling me into an embrace that felt like returning home after a long journey.

"Thanks, I've missed you guys." The words were barely above a whisper, yet they carried the weight of years.

"Missed you more," she quipped, releasing me to hold me at arm's length, her gaze scanning my features. "About time we got together again."

"Yeah, it's been way too long."

"Mom squad, assemble!" Kara called over her shoulder, and soon, I was enveloped by the other mothers. Each hug reignited a flame of camaraderie that had never truly dimmed. Someone handed me a glass of champagne.

"Look at her, all FBI badass," said Jen, squeezing my hand and drawing me into the warmth of the room filled with familiar faces.

"Let's toast to arrivals, new chapters, and old friends," proposed Amy, raising her glass with a flourish that drew us all into a collective lean.

"Old friends," we echoed in unison, the clink of our glasses sealing the sentiment.

"Alright, enough sappiness—let's get this party started!" Kara declared, the twinkle in her eye promising mischief and laughter in equal measure.

"Lead the way," I grinned, following the group deeper into the heart of the main house and into the weekend that lay ahead, ripe with potential. There were a lot of other guests already there, people who knew the birthday boy, Mark, and his mother, faces I had never seen before, and I realized this was a huge event, but how could I be surprised, knowing Victoria, Mark's mother? This was so like her—always going over the top and making it extravagant. Nothing was too big or too much.

I stayed with the women I knew, my old gang. The laughter crescendoed around me. I stood for a moment, my gaze dancing over each animated face—lines of time etched with joy, eyes alight with stories waiting to spill. The air buzzed with an energy that seemed to hum through my veins, reigniting sparks of a life paused but never forgotten.

"Can you believe this place?" Jen's voice cut through the din, her arm sweeping across the scene like a show host unveiling a grand prize. "It's like we've stepped into a Bond movie, minus the espionage… or maybe not?" Her eyebrow arched playfully.

"Speak for yourself," I quipped back. My eyes narrowed mockingly as I scanned the room, playing along. "I'm always on the clock."

"Ah, that's our Eva Rae," Kara chimed in from the other side, her laughter a bright chime. "Always the agent, even when she's off duty."

"Old habits die hard," I admitted with a shrug, feeling the soft fabric of the couch as I sank into it, the cushion embracing me like an old friend. As I settled in, I watched our hostess, Victoria, make her grand entrance. She was draped in a shimmering designer gown that sparkled with every step and was a vision of opulence. Her diamond-studded heels clicked rhythmically on the marble floor, announcing her approach. Her hair was styled in perfect waves, and her jewelry caught the light, casting tiny rainbows around the room.

"Look at us," Victoria sighed, her voice laden with nostalgia, as she plopped beside me with a light kiss hello on the cheek. "Mothers, professionals, survivors of teenage drama—"

Her presence was as luxurious as her surroundings, embodying wealth and extravagance.

"Miracle workers," Michelle interjected, winking from her armchair fortress. "Don't sell us short."

"Indeed." I nodded, warmth spreading through my chest. Our collective journey had been a fabric interlaced with strands of all colors, some dark, others vibrant. Yet here we were, together again, the pattern of our friendship resilient against the years.

"Remember when we thought planning playdates was complicated?" Amy mused, a glass of wine in hand, swirling the ruby liquid like it held our past.

"Ha! Child's play compared to navigating college applications and first heartbreaks," I said, meeting her eyes. There was an unspoken understanding there, a shared battle won.

"Speaking of heartbreaks, how's Matt doing?" Jen's question pierced the light mood, her concern genuine. "We all heard what happened."

"Thriving," I replied earnestly, my thoughts flickering to his smile, the way his determination had conquered adversity. "He's found his calling in cybercrime. And he's got a new leg that's more tech-savvy than my entire office."

"Cheers to that!" they exclaimed in a haphazard chorus, glasses aloft.

"Cheers indeed," I echoed, my voice steady but my heart full. In this room, with these women who had seen me at my best and worst, I felt the world's weight lift slightly from my shoulders.

"Here's to a weekend free from worries," Victoria announced, her tone commanding the room's attention. "To laughter, luxury, and a little bit of drinking."

"Or a lot," Kara quipped, earning a round of knowing chuckles.

"Mostly, to us," I added, standing to join the toast. "To the memories we've made and the ones still ahead."

"Hear, hear!" They raised their glasses higher, and at that moment, the outside world fell away. The mysteries and thrillers of life would wait. This weekend was about connection, gratitude, and the sheer, unadulterated joy of being together.

"Let the celebrations commence," I declared, the finality of my words setting the stage for the weekend that beckoned—a pristine page ready to be written upon with laughter, sunsets, and the incredible ink of enduring friendship.

Chapter 3

I SWIRLED the pale golden champagne in my glass, the bubbles catching the fading light as laughter erupted from the cluster of old friends gathered around me. The crisp, cool liquid was a welcome contrast to the warmth that wrapped around us like a blanket in the luxurious living room of Paradise Key Private Resort.

"Mom!" The voice cut through the convivial chatter, a sharp note of joy unmistakable in its timbre.

Olivia burst into the room, her athletic build propelled forward by an energy that seemed to reverberate off the walls. She was all wide smiles and sun-kissed skin—a sight for sore eyes. She had been gone—away at college for months, the longest we had ever been away from each other. I had missed her terribly.

"Olivia," I breathed, setting down my glass with a soft clink against the tabletop.

"Sorry to interrupt," she said, though her grin told a different story—one where apologies had no real place.

"You can never be an interruption," I assured her, standing to wrap her in a hug that felt like coming home after too long away.

"Look at you! You look amazing; you're glowing." My words were muffled in her short hair.

"Mom, you've no idea how much I've missed you." Her voice vibrated against my shoulder, a tremor of emotion bared only in these safe moments.

"Did you see the bungalow yet?" she asked.

"No, I haven't been back there yet. I think someone took my bag there, though."

"Let's get you settled in," she pulled back, her hands gripping mine with gentle purpose. "Wait 'til you see the bungalow. It's something else."

"Lead the way," I replied.

We navigated through the throng of guests, my daughter's presence like a beacon, guiding me with ease.

"It's right down here."

The path to our cabin wound through a lush maze of tropical flora, the air heavy with the perfume of blooming jasmine. Olivia's stride was sprightly, her excitement manifesting in the animated cadence of her voice.

"Everyone's been amazing, Mom," she said, a laugh threading through her words. "And the snorkeling—God, you should see the reefs!"

"Better than the pictures?" I asked, matching her pace.

"Infinitely." Her eyes sparkled.

"Sounds like paradise found," I quipped, noting the impeccable landscaping that framed our walk.

"Totally," she affirmed. A pair of tiki torches flanked the path ahead, their flames dancing against the onset of dusk.

"Olivia!" The call sliced through the warm air, and there he was: Mark—the birthday boy—emerged from around a bend, sunlight gilding his honey-blond hair. With the confident grace of a panther, he closed the distance between us.

"Mark!" Olivia's face split into a wide grin as they collided in an enthusiastic embrace.

"Look at you two, inseparable as always," I said, my heart warming at the sight.

"Can't help it," Mark responded, his smile reaching his warm brown eyes. "She's the sister I never had."

"Adopted by choice," Olivia added, nudging Mark playfully with her elbow.

"Adoption papers are in the mail," Mark joked.

"Come on, we have to show Mom the view from the bungalow," Olivia urged, linking her arm with mine.

"Prepare to be dazzled," Mark said, leading the way with a sashay that seemed to command the very ground he walked upon.

"Wouldn't dream of anything less," I replied, my attention riveted not just by the grandeur of the island but also by the intriguing dynamics at play among its guests.

Chapter 4

I SLIPPED the keycard that Olivia handed me into the lock of my bungalow, a small click confirming my entry into luxury. We walked inside. Olivia was right. The view over the ocean was beyond spectacular.

"I'm staying in this room," Olivia said, pointing at an open door. "Yours is over here."

The door swung open to reveal a room that was everything I expected it to be. Polished mahogany floors reflected the soft glow of the bedside lamp, and the sheets on the king-size bed whispered promises of silken comfort. I admired the array of fresh fruit and chilled water on the marble countertop.

I immediately felt enveloped in tranquility, the only sound being the distant murmur of the sea. Even the air smelled expensive, infused with a subtle scent of jasmine that seemed to be pumped through the vents.

I barely had time to appreciate the artisan chocolates left on my pillow before Olivia's voice carried from outside my room, "Mom, you'll miss dinner if you don't hurry!"

"Coming!" I called back, slipping into sandals that were more suitable for the evening festivities.

I made my way to the main house where the welcome dinner was unfolding like a scene from a movie. Guests mingled on the expansive deck, silhouettes framed against the setting sun. The clinking of glasses punctuated the laughter that swirled around the gathering as lively conversations took flight. A server offered me more champagne, and I accepted, the bubbles tickling my nose as I surveyed the scene.

"Quite the soiree, isn't it?" a woman who appeared at my elbow said, her voice smooth as velvet.

"I'd expect nothing less from Victoria," I responded, taking in the grandeur of the dining area.

"Indeed," she said, her gaze sharp as she scanned the faces of our fellow guests. "My name is Beatrice. I'm Victoria's sister and Mark's aunt."

"Aunt Bea! I've heard a lot about you over the years. Nice to meet you." I extended my hand to the woman who stood like a pillar of grace in an ocean of casual elegance. She was older than Victoria by about seven or eight years.

"I'm Eva Rae Thomas."

Her handshake was firm, and her steel-gray eyes scanned me with an efficiency rivaling any seasoned agent I'd ever encountered.

"Eva Rae Thomas, the friend from the FBI?"

"The one and only," I said.

"I've heard about you too," she said.

"Only good things, I hope."

Beatrice answered with a light smile.

"It's really nice here," I said, to take the conversation elsewhere. "Beautiful."

"Indeed," she said. "But it's not just the surroundings that make this place special—it also has a lot of history."

"Every good mystery needs a backdrop like this," I quipped, matching her wit.

"Careful, Eva Rae," she warned playfully. "You might find yourself part of the story."

"Wouldn't be the first time," I admitted, the corner of my mouth lifting in a half-smile.

"Enjoy the evening," Beatrice said before gliding away to join another conversation, leaving me to ponder her cryptic words.

"Here's to old friends and new adventures!" Victoria's voice rang out clear as a bell, drawing everyone's attention for the toast. "And to my handsome son's birthday, of course. Happy birthday, sweetie. I can't believe you're twenty now."

"Thank you, Mom," Mark said.

"To Mark," she said.

Glasses raised, we echoed her sentiment, the collective cheer marking the beginning of something memorable—or so we hoped. As the applause subsided, I found myself momentarily caught up in the jubilant atmosphere, the intrigue of the evening palpable.

And that's when I saw him—this extremely handsome man. He stood apart, a solitary figure wrapped in mystery, his eyes observing the interactions around him with a quiet intensity that drew me in. The setting sun cast an amber glow on his face, accentuating the thoughtful expression he wore as if it were his armor.

"Who's the loner?" I whispered to Olivia, nodding subtly toward him.

"Ah, that's Emilio," Olivia shared, her voice dropping to match mine. "He came here with Aunt Beatrice. I'm not entirely sure if he's related to Mark or just a family friend, to be honest. Some say he's Aunt Beatrice's young Latin lover."

"Interesting," I mused, watching Emilio's gaze flit across the crowd with a dancer's poise, deliberate and full of purpose. His presence seemed to weave a silent narrative that begged to be read between the lines.

"There's something about him," I continued, more to myself than to Olivia, intrigued by the enigma standing before me.

"Beats me," Olivia shrugged, her attention already snatched away by Mark calling for her to join him and his friends.

"Excuse me," I said, sliding past a waiter balancing a tray of hors d'oeuvres, my feet carrying me toward the intriguing stranger before I could second-guess the impulse.

"Mind if I join you in the land of observers?" I asked, coming to stand beside Emilio.

He turned, a ghost of a smile playing on his lips.

"I prefer it here," he said, his voice a melody that commanded attention despite its softness. "The view is clearer."

"Clarity is often elusive," I remarked, matching his calm demeanor.

"Especially when one isn't looking for it," Emilio countered, his dark eyes locking onto mine for a moment that stretched long enough to feel significant.

"True enough," I conceded. "Eva Rae."

"Emilio," he introduced himself, though I already knew his name. It was a formality, yet there was a weight to it—a significance he intended.

"Enjoying the party?" I ventured, casting a glance at the chattering guests.

"Observation is a form of enjoyment," he replied cryptically.

"Spoken like someone who knows how to listen."

"Or someone who knows what to look for."

"Are you looking for something?" The question slipped out before I could corral it.

"Perhaps." His answer was a wisp of intrigue, leaving me to wonder at the depth hidden beneath the surface of those two syllables.

"Curious," I murmured, filing away the exchange for later reflection.

"Isn't that what brought you here?" Emilio's gaze was penetrating—as if he could see right through me. "Curiosity as to what your friends have been up to, how successful they have been, what they look like now? Who has aged the worst?"

"Touché," I said with a nod, acknowledging the point well made.

"Mom, come on! Dinner's ready!" Olivia's voice pulled me back from the precipice of the conversation, her enthusiasm a stark contrast to the stillness that emanated from Emilio.

"Coming, sweetheart!" I called back, offering Emilio a parting nod.

"Until next time," I said, stepping away, the curtain falling on our brief act in the night's unfolding drama.

Chapter 5

THEN:

The grains of sand, warm and yielding beneath their bare feet, seemed to sing a melody only they could hear. Sixteen-year-old Isla's fingers were laced with Javier's, the connection as natural as the shoreline merging with the ocean.

"Do you ever wish we could just keep walking?" Isla asked, her voice barely rising above the hush of the waves. "Into the horizon, just you and me?"

"Every day," Javier replied, his eyes glistening with that same untamed joy that danced upon the ocean's surface. "But for now, this stolen slice of eternity is ours. Just you and me."

Isla's heart swelled, brimming with love so potent it threatened to spill over. Here, liberated from prying eyes, she could be who she was meant to be. With Javier, every breath was a silent rebellion against the life of pretense she was shackled to at home. The beach was their sanctuary, where whispered promises weren't muffled by the walls of expectation.

Yet, even as laughter bubbled between them, Isla's mind was

ensnared by the thorns of duplicity. The taste of freedom on her tongue was laced with the bitter knowledge that each step taken in bliss was shadowed by an impending return to a fabricated existence. The thought of returning to that meticulously painted lie that her life had become clawed at her insides, a relentless reminder of the price of her happiness.

"Are you okay?" Javier's voice brought Isla back from the precipice of her worries.

"Yes, " Isla replied, squeezing Javier's hand tighter.

It was a half-truth; she was perfect in this fragment of time with Javier but fractured elsewhere. Yet, a fierce resolve burned within her, a silent oath to safeguard the purest thing she'd ever known. Love, she realized, was worth every mask she had to wear, every act she had to perform.

"Let's not think about later, not yet," Javier said, his thumb tracing circles on Isla's palm. The gesture tethered Isla to the present, to the warmth of the sun on her skin, and the promise in Javier's smile.

"Okay," Isla agreed, allowing herself to be anchored in the now, her worries momentarily drowned out by the haven of Javier's embrace.

Javier suddenly sprinted forward, his curly hair catching the sunlight in a wild dance.

"Catch me if you can!" he called back, laughter weaving through his words.

Isla's heart leaped, and with an exhilarated laugh, she gave chase. Her bare feet pounded against the wet sand, cool water splashing up with every step as the ocean hummed its rhythmic song beside them. The sun kissed her shoulders, and the salty breeze tangled itself in her auburn locks, urging her on.

"Slowpoke!" Javier teased over his shoulder, but Isla was gaining ground, the distance between them closing with each joyful stride.

"I'll catch you!" Isla retorted, her voice breathless with exertion and delight. She pushed harder, reveling in the freedom of the moment—the sheer bliss of being untethered.

As they reached the pier, Javier turned, and Isla crashed into him, both of them tumbling onto the soft sand in a fit of giggles. They lay there for a moment, side by side, looking up at the expanse of sky above, their hands finding each other once more.

But as the laughter faded, Isla's thoughts drifted involuntarily to the world beyond the beach—the one where her mother sat on a throne of expectations. She felt the weight of it then, the pressure to be someone else, someone who fit into the pristine image her mother demanded. It was suffocating, like the tight clasp of a necklace.

Or a chain.

Javier's hand squeezed hers, bringing her back from the brink of that cold reality. "What are you thinking?" Javier asked, his tone soft, eyes scanning Isla's face with concern.

"About the act I have to keep up," Isla admitted, her voice barely above a whisper, betraying the turmoil that bubbled beneath the surface. "With Marcus... with my mother."

The silence stretched between them as they contemplated the charade. Isla could picture it all: the polite smiles, the demure glances, the way she had to fold herself into the mold her mother had cast for her. It was a performance she had mastered, but every scene depleted a little more of the authenticity she craved.

"Hey," Javier said, propping himself up on one elbow, his curls casting playful shadows across his face. "You're stronger than any facade, you know that? We'll figure this out together."

Isla nodded, drawing strength from Javier's unwavering belief in her. It was a lifeline in her internal struggle—a reminder that she wasn't facing this alone. She would maintain the illusion for as long as necessary, but with Javier by her side, she dared to hope for a future where she could live truthfully, unapologetically herself.

Isla's gaze drifted beyond the shoreline, where the waves kissed the horizon in a gentle embrace. The ocean sprawled before her, an endless canvas of blues that mirrored the depth of her yearning for a life unfettered by deceit. As she watched the seagulls wheeling freely above the water, their cries echoing the wild pulse of nature, Isla felt a pang of envy for their untamed existence.

"Freedom looks like that, doesn't it?" she murmured to herself, the breeze tangling through her hair. With Javier beside her, the world seemed so vast, so ripe with possibility. Yet the thought of home constricted around her heart like a vise, each wave rolling in a somber reminder of the duplicity she was bound to sustain.

Sensing the shift in Isla's mood, Javier remained silent, offering only the reassuring pressure of his hand steadying her while the whirlwind of emotions churned within her.

A memory surfaced unbidden, taking shape against the back-drop of her mind's eye—a dinner not long past and the sharp clink of fine china as her mother had her maid set the table with mechanical perfection. Isla could still feel the weight of her mother's gaze, icy and scrutinizing as if looking for any crease, any flaw that might betray the family's pristine image.

"Posture, Isla," her mother had chastised, her voice the very embodiment of control as she appraised her daughter with an unsparing eye. "Remember who you are, who we are. There is no room for error in this house."

The words had fallen like a guillotine, severing Isla's hope for understanding, for acceptance. As she stood there, rigid and compli-ant, Isla had known with a sinking certainty that her mother's love was conditional, a currency traded only for obedience and propriety.

"Promise me, Isla," she had continued, the blue of her eyes hard and cold as the ocean depths. "Promise me you will not bring shame upon us."

And Isla had promised, her voice hollow, even as her heart rebelled silently against the falsehoods that shaped her existence. She had smiled and played her part, all the while knowing that the love she held for Javier, bright and fierce and true, was the one thing she must hide at all costs.

Back on the beach, the sun dipped lower, painting the sky in shades of amber and rose. Isla turned away from the haunting beauty of the sunset, feeling Javier's gaze upon her, full of warmth and unwavering affection. In that look, she found the courage to face another family dinner behind the mask for the glimmer of a future where she could be free—free to love, free to live, and free to be the Isla that only Javier truly knew.

Javier's hand tightened around Isla's, a silent promise that pulled Isla back to the present. The weight of her mother's expectations seemed to lift, if only for a moment, as Javier pulled her closer. Waves lapped at their bare feet, a gentle rhythm that matched the beat of Isla's heart.

"Hey," Javier whispered, his voice a soothing balm. "I told you. I am here for you. We'll get through this together."

Isla studied Javier's face—the wild curls framing his features, the fierce determination in his eyes—and something inside her unfurled, a hope that refused to be quashed by fear or duty. She leaned into the embrace, allowing herself to be enveloped by the love that had become her sanctuary.

"I know," Isla replied, feeling the truth of it deep within her bones. "With you, I can face anything."

They stood there, two silhouettes against the ever-changing canvas of the sky, sharing the kind of silence that spoke volumes. It was in these quiet moments that Isla felt most alive, most herself. Yet, the inexorable march of time waited for no one, and the sun's descent reminded her of the world beyond the beach—the world where she played a part dictated by others.

A world that Javier couldn't enter with her.

Reluctantly, Isla stepped back from Javier's arms, her gaze lingering on the horizon where the last rays of daylight clung stubbornly to the sky. She breathed in the salty air, committing the sense of peace to memory.

"It's time," she said, the words tasting bitter on her lips. "I have to go meet Marcus."

Javier's nod was full of understanding, but the sorrow in his eyes mirrored Isla's own. They exchanged a soft, lingering kiss. As they parted, Isla felt the reassuring pressure of Javier's hand giving hers a final squeeze.

"Remember, love is our rebellion," Javier murmured, courage woven into the very fabric of the words.

"Love is our truth," Isla responded, the conviction in her voice belying the ache of departure.

Turning away, Isla began the walk back, each step heavy with the knowledge of the charade she must continue. But a fierce resolve burned bright within her chest—she would protect this love, their love, at all costs. And with each step, she carried with her the image of Javier standing strong against the fading light, guiding her through the performance she had to give.

Chapter 6
PARADISE KEY, SATURDAY MORNING

THE FIRST RAYS of the Florida sun had just begun to caress the edges of Paradise Key Private Resort when Mark's mother, Victoria, with a furrowed brow, paced along the beach.

"Mark?"

Her voice cut through the silence, each call more desperate than the last. The aroma of freshly baked pastries and sizzling bacon had been intended to rouse her son on his birthday morning, yet the untouched bed had whispered a different story.

He wasn't there.

But where could he be?

"Mark!" she shouted again, her footprints marring the white sand, each step erasing the tranquility that the island promised. The breakfast tray, now abandoned, was meant to be a celebratory gesture from a mother to a son, but reality served a chilling alternative.

She neared the lapping waves, the salt air clinging to her lungs. A gasp escaped her as her eyes locked onto a form bobbing rhythmically in the water. She froze, hope and denial warring within her as the object drew closer.

"Please, no," she murmured, the words barely a breath. Her

heart raced; it couldn't be. Not today, not her Mark. Her hand flew to her mouth, her fingers trembling as if trying to hold back the rising realization.

"Mark!" This time, a whisper, a plea to the heavens to undo what her eyes were seeing.

The waves parted, and a pale hand surfaced. Mark's mother's eyes widened, and the ghastly revelation stole her breath.

"No," she gasped, the syllable splintering into a scream that tore through the early morning hush.

"MARK!"

In the nearby bungalows, the scream knifed through dreams and slumber. Doors burst open, and guests spilled out, all clad in the hurried garb of sleepwear. They flocked toward the source, bathrobes billowing behind them, their bare feet slapping the sand, hearts racing with an unspeakable dread.

"Did you hear that?" The words ricocheted from one guest to another, their voices filled with alarm. "What happened?"

"What is it?" A woman quivered, her face ghost-pale beneath the tropical sun.

"Out there—look!"

They converged at the water's edge where Mark's mother stood, rooted in horror. Her sobs cut through the gathering murmurs as the scene's reality unfolded before their eyes.

"Call for help!"

It wasn't clear who had said it, but the command was urgent and desperate.

"Jesus, Mary... it's his birthday," someone muttered, the words hanging heavy as they took in the sight of Mark's mother, collapsed to her knees in the shallow water, her son in front of her, hands clawing at the wet sand.

"Keep back; give her space!" Another voice tried to assert some control, but panic was a wildfire, spreading fast and uncontrollable.

"Is he—?"

"Shh, don't," a hand clasped over a mouth, stifling the question everyone feared to ask.

"Mark!"

The mother's voice broke again, a jagged shard of glass in the murmur of silk pajamas and cotton robes.

"Get blankets, something warm!" Practicality surfaced through the chaos, but the suggestion felt hollow against the chill that had settled over Paradise Key.

"How would... what could have happened?" Words trailed off, no one daring to finish the thought.

"Quiet!"

It was the loudest command yet. Heads turned to the newcomer, a figure of authority even in her haste. She strode forward, her eyes scanning the scene with a precision that belied her calm exterior.

"Mom!" A young girl's voice, stricken, sliced through everything else as she came running up behind her.

"Olivia, stay back!" The command was sharp but protective.

"Let her come; let her—" Mark's mother reached out, her plea swallowed by a fresh wave of grief. "E-Eva... please...."

"Please, everyone, just... please, stay back," Eva Rae said. The silence that followed was thick, each person wrapped in their own shroud of shock.

"Mark," the mother whispered again, a benediction to the son who'd been the heartbeat of this island paradise, now lying silent in its shallow waters.

Chapter 7

I ARRIVED at the edge of chaos, my heart hammering, yet my mind clear. The early morning sun glimmered off the ocean, an incongruous backdrop to the horror unfolding on the beach. My gaze fixed on the water where a small crowd had gathered, their silhouettes stark against the rising light.

"Step back!"

My voice sliced through the murmurings and sobs, commanding attention as I shouldered my way through the throng of pajama-clad guests. Instincts honed by years of service took over. I scanned the scene: Victoria was crumpled near the shore, her friends were running to her, clutching her, and Mark's lifeless form was bobbing in the gentle waves. Kara, Jen, Amy, and Michelle were all there, and all their eyes were on me.

"Someone call 911," I directed, my eyes never leaving what needed to be done. "Now."

"Already on it," came a shaky reply from somewhere behind me.

"Good." I nodded curtly. "We need to get him out of the water. Carefully. I'll guide his shoulders. Who can take his legs?"

Michelle and Jen stepped forward, Michelle's face set with grim determination, while Jen's was pale and drawn.

"Slowly now," I instructed as we waded into the shallows, my hands steady despite the turmoil inside me. My fingers brushed Mark's cold skin, and I suppressed a shudder.

"On three. One… two… three."

Together, we lifted him, moving toward the beach.

"Get those blankets ready!" I called to the onlookers, who scrambled to obey. As we laid Mark down on the sand, I checked for any signs of life, already knowing it was too late.

"Keep everyone back," I told a lanky teen who seemed eager to help.

My words were clipped and efficient. I surveyed the scene, each detail etching itself into my memory—the way Mark's hair fanned out like a halo, the unnatural angle of his arm.

"Mom?" Olivia's voice reached me, quivering with fear.

"Stay back, sweetheart." My response was automatic, even though my heart broke for the grief she was about to experience.

"Is he…?" Olivia's question hung in the air, unfinished.

"Let's not jump to conclusions," I said, though certainty clawed at my throat. I knew it was too late.

She stared at her friend, shock edged into her face. I needed to help her snap out of it.

"What happened?" The whispered question came from a nearby guest, her eyes wide with disbelief. "Did he drown?"

"We'll find out," I promised, though my mind raced ahead to the investigation that loomed before us. I stared at Mark's throat and saw marks, visible bruises resembling finger marks. I knew in that second that this was no accident. Someone had strangled Mark. There was also a long abrasion on his hand, looking like a deep cut. Had someone tried to stab him, and this was a deflection, and then decided to strangle him instead? Maybe he had put up a fight?

This is not good.

"Mom…." Olivia's hand flew to her mouth, her eyes wide with horror.

Her gaze lingered on Victoria, who now sobbed into the embrace of another woman.

"Keep everyone back," I barked again, the agent in me surfacing despite the tremor in my voice.

I turned toward Mark's friends, who had come to celebrate Mark's birthday. They were a tangle of arms and tears. Their grief was a living thing pulsating through the air.

But Olivia stood apart, her stillness almost more jarring than their wailing.

Chapter 8

THE POLICE BOAT cleaved the still waters, its engine a growling intruder upon the island's calm. I watched from the pier as the officers emerged with brisk efficiency, their movements precise and deliberate. The quiet murmur of the guests behind me faltered, then ceased altogether. It was like watching a play change acts; the scene before us shifted from one of shocked whispers to stark reality.

"Everyone, please gather around!" The lead investigator's voice cut through the tension. He stood on the dock, his posture rigid, the silver badge on his chest glinting in the sun. Gravel crunched beneath his boots as he approached, eyes scanning the crowd with laser focus.

"Sir," I said, moving toward him, "Eva Rae Thomas, I'm an agent with the FBI."

His gaze locked onto mine for an instant that stretched too long. The corner of his mouth twitched, not quite a smile, more a recognition of the dance we were about to perform.

"Ms. Thomas," he nodded, his tone leaving no room for pleasantries. "I'll need everyone's cooperation. Statements will be taken back at the house."

"Of course," I replied, my words clipped. "Just thought you should know—"

"Save it for the statement," he interjected, already turning away from me with a dismissive wave.

"Everyone, please make your way back to the house," the investigator's voice cut through the unease like a knife. He stood with an unwavering posture, his authority unquestionable.

"We'll need to take your statements momentarily."

The guests exchanged hollow glances, their expressions still marred by disbelief. They moved as one somber procession, feet dragging across the sun-warmed stones, the collective weight of shock visible in each step.

I joined the end of the line, my mind racing despite the lethargy around me. My gaze lingered on the investigator, watching him issue orders with mechanical efficiency. My FBI training itched beneath my skin, a silent siren call to action that I was forced to ignore.

"Hey," I murmured to no one in particular, "I could help if they'd let me."

But the buzz of my own thoughts was all that answered back. The breeze seemed to mock me, carrying away any chance I had at influencing the investigation.

"Let's just do what he says," someone ahead muttered. I didn't recognize the voice, but the resignation in it was familiar.

"Sure," I replied, more to myself than them. "Just another day in paradise, right?"

A soft snort from someone nearby told me my dry humor wasn't entirely lost. But the moment was fleeting, and we continued our shuffle toward the main house.

"Detective!" I couldn't help but call out once more, turning to face him. "There's something you should—"

"Inside, Ms. Thomas," he retorted without so much as a backward glance. His hand shot up, palm facing me, a clear stop sign.

"Right," I acquiesced, though every fiber of my being screamed to stand my ground. Instead, I turned away, my frustration simmering just below the surface.

"Stubborn," I breathed out, barely audible over the sound of rustling palm trees.

Inside, I would be just another guest, my insights locked behind the doors of protocol. But as the island's lush greenery enveloped us on our march to the house, I made a silent vow.

"Don't feel too sure of yourself, Detective," I whispered into the wind. "I'll find my way in. I always do."

Chapter 9

THE DOOR to the main house swung open, a silent herald to the collective despair that awaited within. The once-vibrant foyer had transformed into a mausoleum of grief. Mark's friends clung to each other in a tight knot near the grand staircase, their sobs echoing off the high ceilings.

"It can't be real," one of them choked out between tears, her voice barely reaching the rafters. "This can't be happening."

"It has to be an accident," murmured another, her words more of a prayer than conviction.

Mothers with faces etched with lines of worry and sorrow whispered comforts that hung hollow in the air. They reached for tissues from boxes that had appeared as if by magic on every flat surface, dabbing at eyes and noses with delicate restraint.

"Stay strong," Amy said, her hand trembling as she patted Kara's back. "For Victoria. We have to stay strong."

In a shadowed corner sat Olivia. She sat apart from the rest, her knees drawn up, arms wrapped around them like a fortress. Her body swayed ever so slightly, a metronome of internal agony. Eyes fixed on her hands, she traced the lines of her palms, a wordless mantra to keep the turmoil inside her at bay.

"Olivia?" I ventured, my voice slicing through the thick air, a scalpel trying to reach her.

"I'm fine," she clipped back, her eyes betraying the lie. They were turbulent seas, threatening to spill over the levees of her lashes.

"No, you're not; of course, you're not," I pressed, but she only nodded, a jerky motion that spoke volumes.

"I'm here for you," I said, and it was both a promise and a plea.

"I know," she responded, her voice a whisper.

"Let me—"

"Can't," she cut me off, her fingers now weaving an intricate pattern of anxiety on her knee.

"Olivia—"

"Stop." A single word, a dam against the deluge.

I exhaled, tasting the tension that hung between us, a bitter tang on my tongue.

"Hey," I murmured, lowering myself beside her. My arms wound around her, firm and unyielding. "I've got you."

She didn't speak; she just tilted into me, her rigid form softening. The subtle shake of her shoulders eased, and her breaths evened out in slow, measured pulls.

"Mom…." Her voice was a thread, barely there.

"I'm right here." I tightened my grip.

"This feels so unreal," she confessed, her words cracking like thin ice.

"That's understandable." I stroked her hair, lines of strategy and care intertwining in my mind. "But know that you're not alone. We'll get through this. Together."

"I'm scared," she admitted, a fissure in her armor.

"Me too, Olivia. Me too." My response was a whisper, a secret pact between us.

The room's pulse quickened, a living mesh of chatter and stifled sobs. I felt it throb against my temples, a constant reminder of the fragility surrounding us.

"A senseless tragedy," someone whispered, their words laced with disbelief.

"Did anyone see anything?" another voice quivered, searching for a thread of reason in the chaos.

I held Olivia tighter, her body a trembling note in the chaos. A mother first, agent second—but both screamed for action. A balancing act on a wire pulled taut by this morning's horror.

"Mom, what if...?" Olivia's voice trailed off, choked by the unspoken.

"Shh, let's not worry about that now. There are a lot of questions we can't answer yet," I murmured, brushing a kiss atop her head. "Focus on now. It's all we can do."

"But you always find answers. You fix things." Her eyes sought mine, seeking the certainty I wasn't sure I could give.

"Olivia, some things..." I paused, measuring my next words. "Some things are beyond fixing. But understanding them? That's within reach."

"Will they even let you help?" she asked, skepticism threading her tone.

"Let me?" I almost chuckled at the idea. "Since when do I wait for permission?"

"Mom, the investigator...."

"Doesn't know what he's up against," I finished for her, my voice edged with steel. The professional in me clawed for dominance over the maternal shield I had wrapped around us. It was a fight I knew all too well.

"Be careful," Olivia breathed, her grip tightening on my arm.

"Always am." The promise hung between us, as heavy as the storm clouds gathering outside.

"Find who did this," she said, not a plea but a command—my daughter, every bit as resolute as I.

"Watch me." And with those words, I sealed my commitment to the truth—no matter the cost.

Chapter 10

I KEPT HOLDING OLIVIA TIGHTLY, my arms a cocoon around her shivering form. The room's atmosphere was thick, a cocktail of whispers and choked-back tears. My mind raced—how would she cope with Mark being gone? Her eyes, wide orbs of shock, were mirrors to the chaos within as she clung to me.

"Mom," Olivia whispered, her voice barely a tremor. "It hurts."

"Shh, I'm here," I murmured, stroking her hair.

A sudden shift in the room's energy drew my gaze. Mark's mother, Victoria, stormed in, her presence slicing through the crowd like a knife. Her flushed face was a canvas of raw emotion—anger laced with sorrow. Each step was a statement, her grief morphing into something fierce and palpable.

"Where is she?" Her voice cut across the room, edged and brittle.

The crowd parted. I tightened my hold on Olivia, ready to shield her from whatever eruption was about to break. What was going on?

She stopped in front of us.

"Olivia!" The accusation was a blade flung into silence. "You know what happened to him! You did this!"

The room, a hive of low murmurs, fell deathly quiet. Every head swiveled, and all eyes were fixed on the confrontation unfolding before them.

"Absolutely not," I said, rising to my feet. My voice was a rock, unyielding against the accusation. "Not my daughter. My daughter is innocent."

"Then explain why——" Mark's mother advanced, her grief morphed into fury.

I stood firm, cutting across her words. "There's nothing to explain." My stance was unwavering, and the protective barrier around Olivia was as solid as my conviction. I sat down by her, holding her in my arms. "Olivia loved Mark."

Mark's mother was relentless, her voice escalating with each word. "I saw them! Together on the beach, laughing, sharing secrets!" Her finger jabbed through the air, a missile aimed at Olivia. "Last night. Before my son vanished."

"Victoria, please," came a strained whisper from somewhere in the crowd.

"Quiet!" she snapped back, not breaking eye contact. "They were inseparable, and now? Mark is dead, and she's standing here, unscathed! She was the last one to be with him before he… before he…."

Olivia quivered within my embrace, her body folding into itself like a delicate origami figure threatened by the strong winds. She pressed her palms over her ears as if to muffle the sharpness of the accusations, a low keening sound escaping her lips. She began to rock, slowly at first, then with more urgency—a silent scream etched in every motion.

"Enough!" I said, my voice slicing through the tension. "Your words are daggers, and you're only hurting an innocent girl!"

"Olivia, look at me," I coaxed, trying to draw her out of her protective shell. But the shell was hardening, and the girl I knew disappeared inside it, replaced by a fragile creature racked by unseen blows.

"She knows something; I'm telling you!" Victoria continued. "It's all her fault. She hurt him. I know she did. She's not even denying it. I want to hear her say she didn't hurt my son. I want her to say it. But she can't, can she?"

"Stop it!" My voice cracked as I angled my body to shield Olivia from the onslaught. "You're wrong."

Victoria's eyes blazed with a fury that could have set the ocean ablaze. "Am I?" she spat.

The room's atmosphere thickened, tension coiling like a spring. Murmurs rippled through the crowd.

"Your grief has blinded you," I said, struggling to keep my own emotions in check. "You're looking for someone to blame. But my daughter isn't the one. Olivia is grieving too."

"Like hell she is!"

"Mom…." Olivia's voice was a frayed thread, barely audible.

"Enough!" I shot back, my plea barbed with desperation. "Can't you see what this is doing to her?"

Eyes shifted; guests traded glances loaded with doubt and curiosity. Some recoiled from the raw display, hands covering mouths, while others leaned in, ravenous for every morsel of conflict.

"Look at her," I demanded, my voice trembling with contained rage and sorrow. "She's your son's friend, not his killer."

"Friends don't lie!" Mark's mother accused, her voice slicing through the murmured speculations.

"Neither does Olivia," I countered, each word a stone in a fortress around my daughter. "Not about this. Not about Mark."

Heads nodded, some in agreement, some in skepticism. The crowd had become judge and jury, their collective breaths held tight as they awaited the next revelation.

A cold hush fell. The double doors to the grand hall swung open with a purpose that made my heart lurch. Two uniformed officers strode in, their steps echoing against the marble floor of Paradise Key Private Resort's most lavish room.

"What's the situation here?" The taller officer's voice cut through the whispers like a knife.

I tightened my grip around Olivia. She shrank against me, her eyes darting to the imposing figures that now commanded the room's attention. The detective from earlier stepped inside.

"Detective!" Victoria didn't miss a beat. She pushed through the throng of onlookers, pointing an accusing finger at Olivia. "That girl," she hissed, "she knows what happened to my son."

The detective's gaze locked onto Olivia, her innocence under scrutiny. His partner fumbled for a notepad, anticipation etched into his face.

"Ma'am, please, calm down and start from the beginning." The detective's words were laced with authority, but Victoria was a cyclone that refused to be stilled.

"Start with her," she urged, insistent, her voice searing through the space between them. "Mark would still be alive if it weren't for her! She was with him last night. I saw them. In a tight embrace. Kissing. And now he's dead. Now, my son is dead."

Olivia's breath hitched, her body tensing as if bracing for impact. I felt her pulse race, a frantic drumbeat against the silence that had once again claimed the room.

"Is this true?" The detective's question was directed at Olivia, but I answered.

"No," I said firmly, standing between them. "You're barking up the wrong tree, Detective."

"Let's keep this orderly," he replied, unswayed by emotion, his professionalism a stark contrast to the theatrics spiraling around us.

"Orderly?" Victoria scoffed. "My son is dead, and you want orderly?"

"Mrs. Thomas," the detective acknowledged me without taking his eyes off Olivia. "I'll need to speak with your daughter."

The detective's eyes darted from the enraged woman before us to me and back again, his face a mask of professional neutrality. I could almost hear the cogs turning in his mind as he weighed our words against the charged atmosphere.

"Detective, I'm an FBI agent," I cut in, my voice slicing through the tension. "My daughter—"

"Agent or not, your badge doesn't change the facts here," he said curtly, barely blinking.

"Olivia is innocent," I pressed on, my words sharp. "There's been a mistake."

"Everyone's innocent until they're not," he replied, his tone even but his eyes skeptical. "We need to follow every lead, Agent Thomas. You should know this, being an agent and all."

"Leads? He's her best friend! They grew up together. There's no way they could have been kissing. My daughter is gay." My voice rose despite my control, the maternal instinct to protect Olivia wrestling with my trained calm.

"Mo-om!" Olivia said, terrified.

"It's true, isn't it?" I said. "You were just good friends?"

"Friends can hide truths too," the detective murmured, more to himself than to me, a slight crease forming between his brows.

"Olivia, I need you to answer some questions," the detective said, his tone calculated. His eyes softened ever so slightly as they found Olivia's frightened gaze.

"Can't you see she's terrified?" My words lashed out, every muscle in my body coiled and ready to strike. But he was unyielding, his duty clear in his mind.

"Ma'am, it's necessary." His voice carried the weight of authority, but there was a tremor of reluctance that betrayed his understanding of her fragile state.

The room had become a living entity, its breath held tight as the detective stepped closer to Olivia. She looked small, folded into herself like a bird protecting its broken wing.

"Is this really needed now?" I challenged, stepping between them, the shield to her vulnerability.

"It's procedure," he insisted, though his caution spoke volumes. He knew the volatility of the waters he was navigating. "She is most likely the last person to have seen him alive."

"At least take her somewhere private," I said.

"Mom, it's okay," Olivia whispered, her voice a thread of silk that might snap at any moment.

"Like hell it is," I muttered under my breath, but I stepped aside, my presence a sentinel beside her.

"Olivia, where were you last night?" His question hung in the air, each word a stone thrown into the stillness.

"After dinner... I... I walked the beach with Mark like we've been doing every night while here, just as friends, goofing around," Olivia stammered, her hands trembling like leaves in the wind. "And then I went back to bed."

"What time was that? What time did you start walking together?"

"I don't know. Eight o'clock, perhaps?"

"Can anyone confirm that you went back to bed?" The detective's eyes never left her face, always searching for a crack in the facade.

"N-no. My mom was already asleep when I came back."

"And when was the last time you saw Mark?" The detective nodded, scribbling notes in his little black book.

"H-he… at the beach. I left him and went to bed. I assumed he went back to his own bed to sleep. When I woke up this morning, it was because I heard someone screaming."

"I see. And when was this? When did you go to bed?"

"I don't know. Around ten o'clock, perhaps?"

"And did you two fight about anything?" the detective asked.

Olivia looked frightened. "F-fight? What do you mean by that?"

"Did you have any argument, any disputes of any sort?"

A murmur swept through the crowd, the sound of waves crashing against the cliffs of doubt. Whispers curled into the air, each one a viper waiting to strike.

"Enough!" I exclaimed, my voice ringing out, silencing the murmurs. "You've got your answers."

"Agent Thomas, please." The detective's admonition was gentle, a plea for composure.

"Mom." Olivia's hand found mine, her grip fierce. "I'm scared."

"Nothing will happen to you," I promised, my stance rigid against the turmoil of uncertainty. "I'm here."

"All right, Ms. Thomas. We'll stop for now, but we will definitely have to talk to your daughter again." He turned to face the crowd and raised his voice. "My colleagues and I will take everyone's statement about their whereabouts last night and this morning. And no one leaves the island."

The detective closed his notebook, his job done for the moment, but the air remained charged, an electric current running from soul to soul.

"Let's give them some space," he announced to the room, parting the onlookers with a mere suggestion.

The crowd dispersed, even though it felt like their shadows kept lingering over us. And there we stood, mother and daughter, united in a fortress built of unwavering love.

Chapter 11

I WAS HUNCHED over the small desk in my bungalow, the glow from the laptop humming before me as noon crept across Paradise Key Private Resort. The detectives had taken everyone's statements and were now focusing on searching for evidence across the island, blocking off areas where no one was allowed to enter in order to prevent contamination. Meanwhile, they had let us go... for now. I had snuck back to the bungalow to do some research.

My fingers paused on the keyboard, hovering as I scrolled through an old news article detailing the island's dark history. It wasn't idle curiosity that had me digging; it was desperation, a mother's need to shield her daughter from accusations that seemed to breed in the humid air.

"Murder," they whispered behind cupped hands, eyes darting toward Olivia with morbid fascination. And the detective—well, he made it clear that my help was unwelcome. But how could I not intervene when every sideways glance accused my child of being a killer?

"Not my daughter," I muttered under my breath, the words a silent vow. Olivia was no murderer, and I'd stake my career on proving it. Everyone else was still huddled up at the main house, but

I couldn't just sit there and do nothing. I decided to do some digging instead. There was one thing I couldn't seem to get out of my head. Aunt Beatrice had mentioned that the island had a history, and that intrigued me. What kind of history was she talking about?

It didn't take me long to find out. Apparently, there had been another murder on the island some ten years ago, and as I found the articles describing it, I almost lost my breath.

The screen before me displayed the ghostly image of a young girl, who the article said was only sixteen at the time of her death. Her name was Isla, and her last name was Walton.

Walton? As in Mark and Victoria Walton?

I stared at the photo and read further as everything fell into place. Isla was Mark's older sister. She, too, had died on this island.

What in the…?

I kept reading, my heart pounding in my chest. Apparently, she had drowned, just like Mark. But marks on her throat told a story of her being strangled or held down in the water. Water in her lungs told a story of drowning; that was what the autopsy concluded: death by drowning. Marcus Cole, the name attached to her death, had confessed to her murder. He said he attacked her by the cove on the other side of the island in anger because she had cheated on him with someone else. He grabbed her by the throat and strangled her. Then he panicked when he saw her lifeless body and realized what he had done. He felt for a pulse, but she was already dead. He even tried CPR. He stood there for a few minutes, staring at her, trying to figure out what to do. He then threw her in the water, hoping no one would find the body.

Reading this made me stop.

"But why would she have water in her lungs then?" The thought jolted through me with the force of a thunderclap. How? This was basic knowledge. Water doesn't enter the lungs if the person is already dead. Because, if they are no longer breathing when they go into the water, there's nothing to drive water into the lungs. Your lungs have a single tube for both entrance and exit. If water tries to enter, it's blocked by the air already present.

If you drown, on the other hand, you're still trying to breathe, meaning that you're trying to pull air into your lungs and end up pulling in water. Isla's death sounded more like she had been strangled while held underwater.

The inconsistency gnawed at me, a bone thrown to the relentless dog of my analytical mind. Something wasn't right. The confession was off, the details twisted into a shape that couldn't fit within the framework of truth.

"It's impossible," I said aloud, breaking the room's silence. I had to dig deeper and peel back the layers of deception that clung to this case like the stubborn vines along the stone pathways outside. For Olivia. For justice.

"Let's see what else they've got wrong," I whispered, my resolve hardening. The stakes were higher than ever, not just for the truth but for my daughter's future.

Without hesitation, my fingers flew across my phone's screen. I found a familiar name, pressed the call button, and held the device to my ear; the ringtone pulsed like a rapid heartbeat. Questions swirled through my thoughts, each demanding attention.

"Simmons."

"Agent Simmons, it's Eva Rae Thomas." My words cut through the line, urgency underpinning each syllable.

"Eva, to what do I owe the pleasure?" His voice was calm and steady in the chaos. We had worked together for years in the FBI, and I knew I could always trust him to help me.

"I know it's Saturday. But I have an old case that I need to learn more about. Paradise Key. In the Marcus Cole confession, a young boy of only seventeen said he killed his girlfriend, " I said quickly, dispensing with pleasantries. "Something's off."

"Go on," he prompted, interest piqued.

"Marcus claimed he killed Isla before putting her in the water. But she had lots of water in her lungs, and the autopsy said the cause of death was drowning."

There was a pause. A thoughtful hum sounded from his end. "Maybe she wasn't fully dead? Maybe falling in the water made her wake up and breathe in the water?"

"He said he felt for a pulse but found none. He even tried to perform CPR, which tells me he knows how to look for a pulse."

"Mistakes happen in confessions, but you think there's more to it?"

"More than a mistake. I need your insight."

"Alright, let me pull up the file. Give me a sec," he replied, the sound of clicking keys leaking through as he pulled out his laptop.

"Time isn't a luxury we have," I pressed, glancing at the sky outside. "There's been another murder. Same island, same family."

"Really? Now that is suspicious, indeed. Here we are," Simmons said after a moment. "I see what you mean. Discrepancies could point to…."

"Coercion?" I offered.

"Or a cover-up. You thinking what I'm thinking?"

"Someone else is behind this," I affirmed, feeling the sharp edges of a larger conspiracy taking shape. "And that someone just killed again."

"Be careful, Eva. This is big, isn't it?"

"Very big," I admitted. "It involves my daughter now."

"Say no more. I'm in. What do you need?"

"Everything you've got on Marcus Cole and any connections to the island," I demanded, my tone brooking no argument. "Any inconsistencies in the old case."

"Consider it done," he assured me, and I could almost hear the gears turning in his seasoned mind. Simmons was a genius in my book. "You'll have it by morning."

"Thanks, Simmons. I knew I could count on you." My grip on the phone eased slightly.

"Always, Eva. Watch your back out there."

"Will do," I promised before ending the call, determination steeling my resolve.

I stood up, feeling the bungalow walls closing in on me. I had to find and talk to Olivia. Make sure she was okay. As okay as possible. I was worried about her. She left the main house to go for a walk, she said, when I hurried back to my laptop. She hadn't come back yet.

The humid air hit my cheeks as I stepped outside, the tropical paradise suddenly feeling more like a well-manicured prison.

Flip-flops clicking against stone, I marched along the pathway, each step punctuated by the whispers of palm fronds. I used Find My Phone to track her. It usually did the trick. Conspiracy theories chased each other around my mind, demanding attention. They swirled like the breeze, impossible to grasp but undeniably present.

The resort's beauty mocked me; its serenity was a stark contrast to the turmoil within. Worried about my daughter, I picked up the pace, my resolve hardening with every stride. The truth was hidden somewhere among these opulent trappings, and I would tear down paradise itself to find it.

Chapter 12

The golden light of twilight melted into purples and blues as Isla's feet traced a familiar path across the white sands, away from the comfort of Javier's embrace and toward the complexities that awaited her at home. Her heart was so confused. She knew she loved Javier but also knew she had obligations to live up to. Each step was measured, taken with the resolve of someone who knew the road ahead would require every ounce of strength she possessed.

Her thoughts danced between the warmth of Javier's laughter, echoing like a melody in her mind, and the image of Marcus—kind, unsuspecting Marcus—who played his part in a play he didn't fully understand. Even now, as she approached the back porch of the main house, Isla rehearsed the lines of affection she must deliver, a performance devoid of the fire that burned within her whenever she thought of Javier.

"Hey, Isla," came the gentle voice that always seemed laced with hidden sorrow, which Isla knew all too well.

She lifted her gaze to find Marcus leaning casually against the white picket fence, his sandy-blond hair catching the last light of day. His smile was genuine and reached his eyes—a clear blue that held an ocean of kindness. He had dressed simply, in a soft cotton shirt that complimented the ease of his demeanor, yet behind the casual façade, Isla could sense his eagerness to please, to be the perfect accompaniment to the life her mother had envisioned for her. He had arrived at the island a few hours earlier and would stay with them for a couple of weeks. Her mother had invited him. Meanwhile, Javier's mom worked at the resort, and he had gone back to help her out, cleaning the bungalows, as she usually did on Saturdays. Isla didn't understand how it was okay for her to play with Javier when they were children but not okay for her to date him, according to her mother, who had forbidden Isla from seeing him after she caught them kissing in the pantry a year ago. They had known each other all their lives, and it was never a problem for her mother that they hung out together... ever. Not until now. What had changed? Victoria told her then that she wanted her to be with Marcus, and even though he was a nice guy, he was no Javier.

"Marcus," Isla replied, allowing her smile to grace her lips, though it paled in comparison to the one reserved for Javier. "Sorry I'm a bit late. I went for a walk on the beach."

"No problem," he said with a dismissive wave of his hand, his tone light but layered with an emotion deeper than the tranquility he portrayed. "The sunset was worth waiting for, wasn't it?"

"Always is," she acknowledged, her words carrying a double meaning, her mind briefly drifting back to Javier before snapping back to the present.

Marcus stepped forward, offering a supportive arm, which Isla took with practiced ease. They began to walk, their footsteps in sync, creating a harmony that contrasted sharply with the discord in Isla's heart. She knew Marcus harbored feelings for her, deep feelings. And she knew, too, that his willingness to maintain this charade, to be her shield against her mother's scrutiny, was born out of a love that expected nothing in return.

They were the picture of a young couple bathed in the innocence of first love. But beneath the surface, under the calm expression that Marcus wore so effortlessly, lay the truth of their situation —a truth that bound them together in a secret that was both their burden and their bond.

Chapter 13

I ROUNDED the winding curve of the pathway, and there she was: Olivia, elegantly perched on the edge of a sun-bleached lounge chair beside the infinity pool, a shimmering ribbon of water that melded seamlessly with the sprawling horizon. The pool's surface caught the glint of the sun like scattered diamonds while its edge slowly faded into the vast unknown. Her steady gaze remained fixed on that distant point where the sky tenderly embraced the endless ocean, her body coiled with tension as taut as a wound spring.

"Hey," I called out softly, my voice a gentle ripple in the quiet evening air, careful not to disturb her fragile composure.

She did not turn around. "Hi, Mom," came her whispered reply, laced with a reluctance that spoke of hidden turmoil.

"Mind if I sit?" I asked, offering a welcoming gesture toward the now empty chair beside her—a silent invitation mingled with hope.

"Go ahead." Her tone was flat, as though the words themselves couldn't carry the weight of her emotions.

As I eased into the chair, the fabric whispered against my skin, its soft rustle a stark contrast to the charged silence between us—a live wire humming with the raw energy of unspoken fears and buried truths.

"Beautiful day," I ventured, studying her every blink and slightest twitch as if trying to decipher a secret message hidden within her eyes.

"Sure," she replied, her voice barely audible above the gentle, rhythmic lap of pool water against the cool, tiled edge, blending with the ambient murmur of a distant evening breeze.

"Olivia," I said softly, leaning forward with my elbows resting on my knees, my eyes earnest and imploring. "You're like an unread book right now. Please, talk to me."

Her shoulders drooped in resignation. "There's nothing to talk about," she muttered, her posture shrinking into itself as though trying to hide from something unseen.

"Sweetheart, you're like a clamshell locked tightly shut. What's happening inside?" I pressed, my tone tender yet insistent, desperate to unlock the hidden corridors of her mind.

"Nothing I can't handle," she snapped, her eyes flashing with furtive defiance as they finally met mine. Defensive walls rose between us, her gaze full of unspoken narratives her lips refused to unveil.

"Is it about Mark?" I dared to ask, each word heavy with suspicion and genuine concern. "Okay, that was a dumb question."

Her silence was louder than any declaration, a poignant testament to her internal struggle.

"Because if people are whispering—" I began, my voice steady though my heart fluttered with anxiety.

"Mom, stop." A sharp edge marked her tone, her words imbued with a finality that brooked no further intrusion. "Just stop."

"Can't do that," I replied, firmness laced with tenderness, unwilling to let the distance between us widen further. "Not when it comes to you."

"Please." She murmured as she turned away, her face briefly softening into a tender plea before hardening once more.

"Olivia, look at me," I insisted, waiting patiently until those guarded eyes met mine again, clear yet laden with worry. "I know you didn't do it."

"Doesn't matter what you know," she retorted, bitterness

threading through her words like dark smoke rising from a smoldering fire.

"It matters to me. It matters to the truth," I countered softly, each syllable a promise to protect her innocence.

"Let's just drop it, okay?" A veil of resignation fell over her face, her gaze drifting back to the vast, restless waves.

"Can't do that either." I stood up slowly, brushing off the invisible grains of sand clinging to my shorts, my voice laced with determined warmth. "We'll get through this. Together."

"You say that all the time, Mom, yet you know this is my battle —" she began, her voice trembling as she bit her lip, holding back a torrent of pent-up emotion just barely contained under the surface.

"Trust me," I urged, extending my hand. "We'll clear your name. I'm working on it already. I want you to know I'm not just going to sit here and do nothing."

Her fingers quivered before slipping tenderly into mine, a silent pact woven in the space between us.

"Thanks, Mom. I don't mean to be ungrateful. I know you'll do anything for me. It means a lot to me."

"Come on," I said, gently drawing her up and guiding her away from the edge of despair. "Let's head back."

Together, we walked along the stone path back to the bungalow, side by side, yet feeling like we were traversing separate universes. Each step was filled with the weight of doubts and the murmur of dark possibilities.

There was a murderer on this island, and we were all stuck there until it was discovered who it was.

Chapter 14

LATER, I pushed open the hefty mahogany door of the main house, the hinges silently yielding to my entrance. I had left Olivia at the bungalow, not wanting her to be around people who were treating her like a pariah.

The air was thick with tension like a heavy curtain that refused to sway even as the breeze from the ocean teased its edges. Guests huddled in clusters, their murmurs ebbing and flowing with the secrets that Paradise Key Private Resort seemed to swell with.

"Ms. Beatrice," I called out, my voice slicing through the low hum of conversation as I approached her solitary figure by the grand bay window. Her posture, a column of icy detachment, remained unaffected by the collective anxiety of the room.

"Agent Thomas," she greeted without turning, her gaze fixed on the horizon beyond the glass.

"Enjoying the view?" I asked, matching her coolness note for note.

"Always," Beatrice replied, sparing me a glance now, her eyes sharp and assessing. "Though one wonders if there's more to see than meets the eye."

"Speaking of which," I leaned in, lowering my voice just enough to be conspiratorial, "I can't help but notice your sister's... let's call it disinterest in your friend Emilio."

"Is it that apparent?" She turned fully toward me, an eyebrow arching with practiced control.

"Only to a trained eye," I said. "Care to share why?"

"Does an aversion need justification?" Beatrice countered, her lips twitching into a half-smile that didn't reach her eyes.

"Maybe not, but it could be important," I pressed on.

"Then let's say she and Emilio have different ideas about a lot of things," she offered, her words measured, her tone laced with something unreadable.

"Could you be more specific?" I asked.

"Some subjects are more controversial than others."

"Controversial enough to kill for?" I watched her closely.

"Agent Thomas," she sighed, finally facing me again, "one hopes that in the world of civilized beings, we can resolve our differences without resorting to barbarism."

"Yet here we are," I pointed out, "on an island where civilization seems to have taken a back seat to murder."

Beatrice's gaze slipped past me, landing on a distant point of the room.

"Human nature is complex."

She paused, selecting her next words with surgical precision. "Aesthetic disagreements can be... let's say about the color of one's skin."

"Emilio's skin?" I pointed out.

"Indeed," she said smoothly. "My sister has a... let's say... aversion to anyone bringing dark-skinned people into the family."

"I see."

I pocketed her cryptic hint like evidence and shifted my focus across the room. Victoria, Mark's mother, was engaged in a fiery exchange and flicked her hands in sharp gestures. Her voice pierced the hum of conversation, each syllable spiked with venom.

"Can you believe the audacity?" she spat, unaware of my approach. "Bringing him here?"

"Hardly surprising," the other guest muttered, leaning in. "Beatrice must have an agenda."

"Agenda?" I interjected, sidling up beside them. Their heads swung toward me like startled deer clocking an intruder.

"Eva Rae," Mark's mother greeted me, her voice dropping to a cooler octave. "We were just—"

"Discussing Emilio?" I finished for her. "I'm curious about this agenda you mentioned."

"Curiosity," she quipped, "can be a perilous pursuit."

"Perilous but necessary," I replied, locking onto her evasive stance. "Especially when agendas turn fatal."

"Fatal? Pfft," she scoffed, dismissing the idea with a wave. "Emilio is… misguided, not murderous."

"Yet here we stand, at a murder scene," I reminded her, leaving the statement hanging like a noose. "And there's a man present you don't care for and obviously didn't want here."

"Coincidence, Eva Rae," she insisted, but her eyes darted away, telling a different story.

"I don't believe in coincidence," I shot back.

"Coincidence or not," the other guest chimed in, "it's clear that Emilio's presence has stirred troubled waters."

I squared my shoulders.

"Your relationship with Emilio," I started, casual but piercing. "It goes back?"

"Years," she clipped out, her eyes narrowing just enough to betray her guard.

"Where do you know him from?"

"Oh, I barely remember anymore. You know how it is, Eva Rae."

"Are you sure? Then why are you unhappy with him being here?"

"Let's just say my sister wasn't exactly honest about the person she wanted to bring here for my son's birthday—about his background, where he came from, and who he was." Her tone was dismissive, but her fingers betrayed her, tapping a nervous rhythm on her forearm.

Was she referring to the fact that he was Hispanic? I had known Victoria for years and never heard her say anything remotely racist.

"What happened to your daughter? To Isla?"

Her tapping stopped. Silence hung between us, heavy and expectant.

"You've lost two children now," I said. "Here on the island."

She looked at me, confused. Tears sprung to her eyes, but she refused to let them escape and turned away instead.

"I need to… I have to…."

She walked off, stoic as always. Amy came up to me. "Why did you have to mention that? Marcus Cole committed that murder. He was sent to jail for it."

I nodded, breathing heavily, reminding myself I was among friends here. Good friends. Old friends.

Yet I never knew that Victoria had a daughter. I guess we weren't as close as I thought.

Chapter 15

THE DOOR SHUT FIRMLY behind me, cutting off the low hum of hushed conversations and clinking glass as I left the main house. I glanced over the expansive view of the ocean visible through the large windows. There, standing alone on the beach against the horizon, was Emilio.

Alone.

"Evening, Emilio," I said as I approached, my footsteps muted on the warm sand.

"Agent Thomas," he replied without turning around, his voice deep and steady.

"Beautiful view," I commented, pausing beside him.

"Calm on the surface, but it hides strong undercurrents," he said, watching the rolling waves.

"Like this island," I ventured, matching his metaphorical tone.

"Exactly." He finally faced me, his gaze scrutinizing. "You're here for answers, aren't you?"

"Answers lead to truth," I stated, studying the guarded look in his eyes. "Isla's truth."

Emilio paused, then slowly nodded.

"So, you've heard. Yes, I knew Isla. She had many sides—some clear like these waters, others less so."

"Was your friendship with her straightforward or complicated?" I asked, implying the underlying tension without mentioning my own uncertainty.

"Both," he admitted, a hint of sadness in his voice. "She trusted me until things turned complicated."

"Turned complicated? How?"

"Problems arose," Emilio said shortly.

"Between you two?"

"Between all of us," he corrected, gesturing toward the house. "This place is built on complex relationships."

"Care to elaborate on those 'complications'?" My tone was steady, but inside, my mind raced.

"Another time, perhaps," he said, his eyes flickering with unreadable emotion. "Ask Mrs. Walton. She knows more than anyone else around here."

"Thank you, Emilio." I nodded, respecting his boundary while filing away every nuance.

"Remember, Agent Thomas," he called as I started walking away. "In tough situations, it's not just about getting by—it's about knowing where you're headed."

His words stayed with me as I paused briefly, nodding in agreement. I let his advice sink in, each word pushing me further into the heart of the investigation. A family's future was at stake, and mine as well.

"Complications," I muttered, the word bitter on my tongue.

It hinted at more than just disagreements—it might even point to motives for murder.

I glanced back at the main house, realizing that every person there was potentially hiding secrets behind polite smiles and casual talk.

Chapter 16

I PERCHED on the edge of a plush armchair, the muted hues of the bungalow around us doing little to brighten the mood. Across from me, Olivia sat huddled into herself, her eyes anchored to the floor. Each second stretched, taut with her silence.

"Olivia," I began, tilting my head to catch her gaze. "Talk to me. What happened last night? I have a feeling there's something you haven't told me. Something important."

She didn't look up, didn't waver. Her silence clung to the air like the humidity outside these walls.

"Sweetheart, I need you to tell me." My voice softened, but beneath it lay the unmistakable firmness honed by years in the field. "It's important."

"Mom...." The word barely escaped, a whisper lost in the vast room.

"Whatever it is, we'll handle it, sweetie. I can handle it." I reached across the divide, a mere two feet that felt like miles. "I don't believe you could ever harm your best friend."

Olivia's breath hitched, her fingers tightening around the fabric of her jean shorts. She shook her head, a slight, almost imperceptible movement. It broke my heart to see her in this state. My Olivia, my child.

"Olivia." I leaned in closer, urgency threading through my tone. "This isn't just about you or me. It's bigger. You know that."

Silence was her shield, but I saw its cracks. The tremor in her hands. The quick dart of her eyes.

"Please," I implored, the investigator giving way to a mother's plea. "We're running out of time. The police are investigating this now as a murder case, and you're their prime suspect. You were the last person we know of to have seen him alive."

Her lips parted, then sealed once more. A battle waged in those depths I knew so well. Her eyes flickered—defiance, fear—emotions I couldn't let solidify into an impenetrable fortress.

"Olivia," I started again, my tone a blend of steel and silk. "Why won't you talk to me? Why won't you tell me what happened? What are you afraid of?"

She didn't respond; her gaze was glued to the floor, but I sensed the churning beneath her stoic exterior—it was time for a different approach.

"Remember the summer at Camp Blue Ridge?" I asked.

A slight twitch of her eyebrow—that was all—but enough to tell me I had struck a nerve.

I took us back, two years past, to a moment etched in memory. Olivia had returned from camp quieter than when she'd left, a hurricane brewing behind her eyes. Late one night, I found her on the porch, her knees drawn up to her chest.

"Can we talk?" she had whispered then, her voice trembling like leaves in a soft breeze.

"Always," I had replied, sitting beside her, our shoulders nearly touching.

"Mom, there's this girl...." The words had come out hesitant, testing the waters between us. And that's when I knew. My daughter had fallen in love with a girl. It took her years to gather the courage to tell the rest of her family and friends.

"Tell me about Mark," I said now, grounding myself in the present as I watched the flicker of recognition in Olivia's eyes.

"Did something happen with Mark last night?" I probed gently. "Is that why you won't talk about it?"

She glanced up, then away, a flash of the confusion and fear I remembered from that summer's confession.

"Being judged is the least of your worries," I assured her, though my heart raced with concern for what remained unsaid.

"Is it?" she muttered, almost too quiet to catch.

"Absolutely."

"Then why do I feel like it's everything?" Her voice cracked, revealing the turmoil within.

"Because it feels personal. Intimate." I kept my tone measured, recalling the courage it had taken her to confide in me back then.

"Mom, I'm gay, and you know it," she finally said, her voice a whisper against the weight of secrets. "You wouldn't understand."

"Then help me understand," I urged, leaning closer, willing her to trust me with whatever haunted her from the shadows of the night before. But she remained silent, and then my phone rang.

Chapter 17

THE VIBRATION WAS SUDDEN, a subtle intrusion. I excused myself with a nod to Olivia and fished the phone from my pocket.

"Matt," I answered, stepping away from my daughter.

"Hey, Eva Rae." His voice held the steadiness of bedrock, yet I could hear the edges fraying with concern. I had filled him in on what was going on when speaking to him earlier. I could tell by the tone of his voice that he was worried. "How's it going down there?"

"Slow," I admitted, watching Olivia through the slats of the plantation shutters. "Like trying to piece together a jigsaw with half the pieces missing."

"Sounds about right," he chuckled softly. "How's Olivia holding up?"

I sighed. "Hard to tell. She's still not talking about what happened, and it's driving me nuts."

"Keep at it. She'll confide in you when she's ready. If there's anyone she will ever talk to, it's you. You two have always been close."

"I know. It just... well, it hurts seeing her this way, this tormented. And if I'm being honest, it breaks my heart that she doesn't feel like she can tell me. How are things at home?"

"It's a bit of a circus back here without you. Alex tried to use the blender, turning the kitchen into a makeshift tropical smoothie bar —minus the cups."

"Classic Alex." The image brought a reluctant smile to my lips despite the gravity of my situation.

"Yeah, and Christine is convinced she's the next master chef. She wants to cook dinner for us. I'm getting the fire extinguisher ready as we speak."

"Brave man." I matched his lightness, a counterbalance to the weight pressing on my chest. "Anything else?"

"Angel's struggling, Eva."

The words rippled through me like a cold current. I leaned against the wall of the bungalow.

"Still having nightmares?" My voice was a mere whisper.

"Every night." Matt's voice cracked like the surface of a frozen lake underfoot. "She cries for you and Olivia. She keeps asking when you're coming home."

A mother's guilt clawed at me, sharp and unrelenting. "I'm working on it," I said, the promise steeling my resolve. "I'll fix this."

"I know you will. And I don't mean to rush you; I just want to let you know you're missed. But take care of our girl first, Eva." The softness in his plea wrapped around me like a lifeline. "We need you both safe."

"Of course." I pressed my fingertips to my temple, willing strength into my bones. "I'm doing everything I can."

"I know you are."

"Give Angel a kiss from me, will you? Tell her... tell her Mommy's catching the bad dreams."

"Will do."

He paused, and even without seeing him, I knew he was wearing that half-smile, which was all reassurance and heart. "Get back to us soon, superhero."

"Count on it."

I ended the call, tucking the phone away with a newfound urgency pumping through my veins. Angel needed me. Olivia needed me. I could only be in one place. Time was slipping through my fingers.

I needed to step up my game.

Chapter 18

I SAT DOWN NEXT to Olivia, the plush chair cushion yielding to my weight. The scent of salt and hibiscus breezed through the room. I needed her to see me, not just as an FBI agent or a worried mother.

"Olivia," I began, my voice even, "when I was about your age, I faced something... it nearly broke me."

Her attention drifted from her hands, a slight tilt of her head. It was the smallest window, but enough for me to slip through.

"Back then, I had a friend. He was more than a friend, really." My heart hammered from the emotions I'd locked away. "You know the story, or at least some of it. It was actually Matt. We were childhood friends."

Her eyebrows knitted together, curious despite herself.

"Everyone thought we were just close. Best friends till the end, you know. But it was more. I already had feelings for him, but I was terrified." I paused, swallowing hard. "Terrified of him not feeling the same, of losing him as a friend."

"Mom...." Olivia's voice was a feather, soft and uncertain.

"Olivia, I buried those feelings so deep that I convinced myself they weren't real." I reached across, my fingertips brushing hers. "I left town and met your dad. It wasn't until I returned many years later that I finally reconnected with those feelings. They had been there all the time. But we lost many years."

She looked up now, her guard momentarily down. Eyes wide, searching mine for the truth.

"Did you ever tell him back then?" Her voice was stronger, emboldened by my admission. "How you felt?"

"No." A heavy word laden with sadness. "And that's my biggest regret."

"Because you were scared?"

"Because I let fear dictate my life." I held her gaze, steady as the ground beneath us. "Don't make my mistakes, Olivia. Don't live with 'what ifs.'"

Her breath caught, and the flicker in her eyes ignited a spark of understanding. The connection was tenuous, a thread strung between us, but it was there.

"Mom, I—" she started, then stopped, the words catching in her throat.

"Whatever it is," I encouraged, "you can tell me."

Olivia's fingers twitched, the only tell of her inner chaos. "I just... I don't know where to start or how to explain it.

"Start anywhere," I replied, my voice low. "Start with one thing."

She bit her lip, the quiet stretching taut between us.

"Mark and I—we..." she faltered, and her eyes darted away.

"Olivia." My tone sharpened, not with reprimand, but with urgency. "Trust me."

Her gaze snapped back, meeting mine. "We walked the beach every night. We talked and goofed around like old times. I promise that's all it was—us being like we used to be together. And then—"

"Then what?" I pressed, leaning closer.

"Someone saw us!" The words spilled out, frantic. "They threatened Mark."

"Who?" My mind raced, wheels turning, piecing together shadows of the threat. "Why would they threaten him?"

"I don't know!" Her distress was palpable, her voice rising, thin and strained. "He wouldn't tell me who it was or why. But it made him really worried for some reason."

"Shh." I reached out, stilling her trembling hands with my own. The contact grounded us both. "We'll find out."

"But it's all messed up now!" Tears brimmed in her eyes, her fear naked and raw. "People think I killed him!"

"Listen to me," I said, every word deliberate, honed by years of crises. "Nothing is beyond repair."

She swallowed hard, nodding, clinging to the promise like a lifeline.

"Mom, I'm scared," she whispered.

"Scared is okay," I reassured her, my voice even. "Only when we're scared can we do something brave. It wouldn't require courage if we weren't afraid to do it."

Her breath hitched, and she nodded, a mute agreement to the unspoken pact between us. I felt my heart ache for her and knew that no matter the darkness lurking, no matter what truths were hidden in silence, I would shield her.

Chapter 19

THEN:

Isla's fingers curled around Javier's, their hands swaying gently between them as they walked along the shoreline. Each step imprinted a fleeting memory in the wet sand, one that the ocean would soon claim. Isla's laughter mingled with the rhythmic whisper of the waves, her voice a melody of contentment.

"Imagine it, Javier," Isla said, her eyes reflecting the horizon's infinite promise. "A little studio overlooking the ocean, where you can paint, and I can write, and nothing but the sound of the surf to break the silence."

Javier squeezed Isla's hand, his smile as radiant as the dreams they wove. "With mornings spent chasing the dawn and evenings capturing the sunset on canvas," he added, his words painting an idyllic future that danced before Isla's imagination like a treasured mirage.

The ocean breeze played with strands of Isla's hair, teasing them into a wild dance that mirrored the untamed spirit within her. The sun dipped lower, its golden light bathing the beach in a warm embrace that seemed to approve of the lovers' plans.

"Freedom tastes sweeter with you," Isla murmured, leaning into Javier. The world beyond their secluded paradise was a distant thought, held at bay by the serenity that enveloped them.

Javier tipped his head back, allowing the breeze to carry away the echoes of his joyous laughter. He turned to Isla, his eyes alight with the fires of a thousand sunsets. "We'll make it happen, Isla. Our own little corner of the world."

The tranquility of the moment wrapped around them, a stark contrast to the silent undercurrent of tension that awaited in the wings—a reminder that their shared dream was as fragile as the shifting sands beneath their feet.

And that's when they saw her.

The horizon, once a canvas of tranquil blues and oranges, was slashed by the dark outline of a solitary figure. Victoria Walton's silhouette stood as if etched into the sky, her posture rigid with purpose.

Isla's heart faltered, a cold thread of recognition winding its way through the warmth of the shared confidences with Javier. The sense of freedom that had buoyed her moments before now felt like a cruel illusion.

Javier's voice trailed off, his gaze following Isla's as it fell upon the unwelcome apparition that advanced toward them with relentless determination. The ocean breeze, which had been a gentle caress, now felt like the foreboding touch of an unseen omen. Isla could feel Javier's fingers tighten around hers.

"Mom," Isla whispered, the word a shard of ice in the balmy air.

Victoria's stride was measured but swift, a metronome ticking toward their inevitable confrontation. With each step that closed the distance between them, the joyful light in Javier's eyes waned, replaced by an understanding of the gravity that bore down upon them. Their haven was breached; their secret was exposed beneath the scrutinous gaze of the matriarch who ruled their world with an iron fist veiled in velvet gloves.

"Explain yourselves," Victoria commanded, her voice slicing through the sound of the waves.

Her ice-blue eyes were twin flames of indignation, the setting sun casting sinister shadows across her immaculate features. "What is this disgrace?"

The accusation hung heavy in the salt-kissed air, a tangible weight that sought to crush the defiance swelling within Isla. She stood rooted to the spot, her mother's presence an immovable cliff against which her desires crashed helplessly. The golden glow of the beach had become a harsh spotlight, illuminating their private rebellion for the world—and most importantly, for Victoria—to judge.

Isla's heart stuttered in her chest, the rhythm of fear tangling with the pounding surf. She could see the anger rising in her mother's eyes, a hurricane of disapproval threatening to sweep away everything she held dear.

"Mom, please," Isla choked out, the words barely a whisper over the ocean's roar. "It's not what you think."

Her mother's glare hardened as if sculpted from the very cliffs that lined their family estate. Isla searched desperately for the right words, the incantation that might dissolve the barriers between them. She felt Javier's presence at her side, a silent pillar of strength in the swirling chaos.

"Javier is important to me, more than you can imagine," Isla continued, her voice gaining volume, each syllable a tremulous note strung upon the thin wire of her resolve. "We love each other, and that love isn't something to be ashamed of—it's beautiful."

Victoria's posture was a portrait of rigid indignation, her silhouette like a dark sail against the bright canvas of the sky. Her voice rose, a crescendo mirroring the gathering swells, each word a crashing wave meant to erode Isla's defiance.

"Betrayal!" Victoria spat out, the accusation sharp as shards of glass. "You dare bring dishonor upon our family? Upon me?"

The raw power of Victoria's ire whipped around them like a gale force wind, her words lashing at Isla's spirit. "You are no daughter of mine if you choose this—this charade over the life I've built for you!"

"Mom," Isla implored, her fury rising within her. "It's not a charade. It's who I am. Javier is part of my life—my heart—and I won't let your prejudices tear that away."

Victoria's face was an alabaster mask, the softness of a mother's love eroded by her relentless convictions. The threat hung between them, an ominous cloud on the horizon:

"Choose him, and you lose everything—your inheritance, your name, your place in this family."

Each word was a thunderclap, echoing the finality of a judgment passed. But even as they fell, Isla stood firm, defiant against the wrath.

Javier's figure emerged from the maelstrom of emotions, his poise undiminished. He stepped forward, a shield wrought from conviction and love, positioning himself between Isla and Victoria's anger. The sunlight caught his curls, setting them ablaze with defiance as he faced the woman who sought to dismantle their world.

"Mrs. Walton," Javier said, his voice a resonant chord that refused to waver under scrutiny. "Love isn't a choice or a mistake—it just is. And it has made Isla stronger, braver, more herself than any other force in this world."

Victoria's eyes narrowed, icy and unyielding, as she regarded the young man who dared to challenge her. Her lips twisted into a semblance of a smile devoid of warmth as she prepared to unleash the full extent of her authority.

"Javier," she began, each syllable dripping with disdain. "You are a temptation in my daughter's life, but it ends here. You were nothing but a fling, a toy to her. It's over now."

She drew closer, her presence oppressive, the air thick with tension. "You will cease this… infatuation immediately. Isla will have no further contact with you. This is my final word."

The gravity of her ultimatum descended upon them like a shroud, its weight heavy enough to suffocate dreams and smother hope.

Isla's fingers clenched into the fabric of her sundress, the soft cotton twisting like the knot in her stomach. Her mother stood before her, an imposing figure against the endless expanse of the ocean, and Isla felt small, her voice barely more than a whisper carried away by the wind.

"Mother, please," she implored, the desperation evident in her trembling words. "Don't do this. Javier—he's everything to me. You have to understand, I love him. What's wrong with that? We have known each other forever. We played together as children here. His mother works for us. I love him. I think I have always loved him. What can be so wrong with that? Can't you be happy for us? For me?"

Her eyes brimmed with tears, daring to spill over as she searched her mother's face for a sign of compassion. At that moment, Isla was stripped bare, her heart exposed, vulnerable to the disapproval she knew was brewing within her mother. The depth of her emotion was palpable, a raw display of longing and affection for the boy who had become her world, her sanctuary from the expectations that were chaining her down.

"Love?" Victoria repeated, the word laced with scorn. Her lips set in a firm line, her gaze cold as the ocean depths. The sun, which had once cast a golden glow upon them, now seemed to highlight the ice in Victoria's veins, the unyielding nature of her resolve.

"I know what is best for you, Isla."

Her voice was a blade of steel slicing through the air. "This... infatuation, it will pass. It's a phase, like so many other things. Like when you played the piano, huh? Remember that? Or when you just had to start playing volleyball, but quit after two weeks. You're a child, a teenager. You don't know what love is. You will thank me one day."

"Please, Mom, please try and understand...."

Isla's plea hung between them, fragile as a seashell, crushed by the sheer force of Victoria's authority. There was no room for nego-tiation in her mother's world, no space for the kind of love that didn't fit within the pristine edges of their family's facade.

"Enough!" Victoria commanded, every syllable a nail in the coffin of Isla's hopes. Her presence loomed over them both, a testament to the power she wielded, the control she clung to with a fervor born of fear—fear of scandal, fear of deviation from the path she had so carefully constructed.

"I refuse to stand here and watch you ruin your life. Your future is not with him," Victoria said, her decision etched into the lines of her face, immutable as the rocks that bordered the beach. She grabbed Isla by the arm and started to pull her away.

"It never can be."

Chapter 20
PARADISE KEY - SUNDAY MORNING

I LEANED against the veranda railing, my gaze sweeping over Paradise Key Private Resort's splendor. It was morning again, and I had barely slept. Olivia finally fell asleep around four a.m., so I let her sleep a little longer while I went out for breakfast. The rustle of palm trees and the distant murmur of ocean waves usually brought a sense of peace. Not today. My chest tightened as I entered the main house.

The grand foyer opened before me, sunlight streaming through the windows and casting long shadows across the floor. With each step toward the breakfast buffet, I scanned faces, analyzed postures, and listened for hesitations in voices that might betray nerves or guilt.

"Ms. Thomas, enjoying your stay?" Mr. Harrison, the resort manager, greeted me with practiced charm. It was routine for him, a question he obviously always asked guests in the morning.

"Not really," I replied, matching his grin while my mind worked double time. "With everything that's been going on. But I have noticed that you run a tight ship here."

"Only the best for our esteemed guests." He puffed out his chest like a proud peacock.

"Indeed." I let the word hang, then moved on. "Say, how long have you worked here, if you don't mind me asking?"

"Oh, we're coming up on fifteen years, me and the wife."

"I see," I said. "So, you live here?"

"We do. No better place in the world."

"And you were here when Isla Walton was found murdered?" I asked.

He took a deep breath and shook his head. "Yes, such a terrible, terrible tragedy. And now it's happening again. We have known the Waltons for many, many years and never thought we'd see this happen to them again."

"And Mr. Walton, he died five years ago, am I right?"

"That is correct, yes. Heart attack as we understand it."

"Yeah, that's what Victoria told me, too. Did you know Isla well?" I asked.

"She would come here every summer when she was out of her boarding school. I believe she went to school in England. She preferred it here to being up north. Didn't do well with the cold, I take it."

That's why I didn't know about her.

"And the boy, Marcus Cole, who was convicted of killing her, did you know him?" I asked.

"Most certainly. He would also come here to visit every summer. They were the loveliest couple. A very good fit for one another, in my opinion. And Ms. Victoria seemed to think so, too. She was very fond of him, even though he came from a different background than Miss Isla. She very much encouraged their relationship. It's very strange what happened. He was such a nice young man. It makes one think... who can you really trust? Especially around your children."

"I guess," I said.

One of the staff members approached him and asked him a question.

"If you'll excuse me," he said and left.

"Of course."

I walked to the buffet and got a plate of scrambled eggs and sausages while thinking about what Mr. Harrison had told me. I sat down, a lot going through my head.

Marcus Cole, who was this guy? This morning, I received an email from Agent Simmons telling me Marcus had recently been released from prison. I couldn't stop thinking about it. The questions darted through my mind. It could be him again. Marcus had reason enough: revenge, perhaps, or a twisted homecoming. With its isolation and luxury, the island presented the perfect stage for either.

Slipping away from the whispering voices and clinking silverware, I made my way toward the bungalows. The breeze tousled my hair, whispering secrets as I passed. Each step was light, a dance with danger on this island masquerade.

"Going somewhere?" A voice sliced through my focus like a knife. It was Michelle. I had walked right past her, caught up in my thoughts.

"Just getting a quick breath of fresh air," I said without breaking stride. My heartbeat thrummed in my ears, a steady rhythm pushing me forward. Michelle gave me a strange look like I was up to no good, but I didn't let it bother me. In front of me loomed the bungalows like pearls on a string. There were thirty-four of them, but only twenty-eight were being used for this event. Six of them remained empty.

Compelled by curiosity, I walked toward the empty ones.

The first bungalow loomed, its door ajar. I paused, listening, then slipped inside. The room was dim, curtains fluttering slightly. I scanned for disruptions, for anything out of place. My hand grazed the bedspread—crisp, untouched—then moved on.

Second bungalow, same routine. Nothing.

But the third... something felt off. No ransacked drawers or scattered belongings. Yet there it was—a small backpack on the floor, a silent scream in the silence. I picked it up. There were a couple of T-shirts and some underwear in it.

Men's underwear.

Stepping out of the bungalow's shadow, I nearly collided with Jason, one of the resort's gardeners. His hands were dark with soil, and a gentle smile played on his lips.

"Ms. Thomas, beautiful day, isn't it?" he greeted, tilting his head.

"Yes," I replied, my eyes not meeting his but darting past to the thickening foliage around us. "You've been here all morning?"

"Since sunrise," he nodded, wiping his brow with the back of his hand. "Keeping paradise perfect."

"Anyone... out of the ordinary cross your path? New faces, maybe?" I kept my tone light, almost idle.

"Here?" He chuckled. "Guests come and go, but today, no new footprints in my gardens."

"Footprints, you say?" I arched an eyebrow, feigning curiosity.

"Metaphorically, Ms. Thomas. Everyone stays on the paths, as they should." He gestured to the neatly outlined walkways.

"Of course," I murmured. My gaze fixed on a crushed frangi-pani flower by the path—a misstep gone unnoticed.

"Anything else, ma'am?" Jason asked, ready to move on.

"Nothing. Thank you," I said, watching him return to his pruning.

I turned away, every sinew taut, every nerve firing. The back-pack, the crushed flower. Something was up.

"Olivia," I whispered to myself, reminding myself of my silent vow to protect her at all costs.

Chapter 21

I WAS on my way back to the bungalow when I heard something. A twig snapped. My head whipped around, eyes narrowing as I scanned the bushes bordering the path, then followed the rustling of leaves under stealthy movement. I held my breath.

"Hello?"

There was no answer but the hush of foliage parting in reticence. A shadow shifted—the briefest flicker of a presence—and then stillness returned, oppressive and mocking. My heart thudded a warning, adrenaline flooding my system.

Another rustle. I halted and put a finger to my lips out of habit. My eyes darted across the underbrush, every training protocol etched into my muscles, tensing for action. There was no breeze to excuse the movement, no benign wildlife to be seen scampering. This was deliberate and calculated.

Was someone following me?

"Show yourself," I demanded, voice steady despite the drumbeat of my heart against my ribs. Silence answered, defiant and stretched thin like a wire about to snap.

I crept forward, one cautious step after another, the crunch of my flip-flops on the ground seeming deafening in the hush.

Another rustle—closer this time, a whisper of sound in the stifling quiet. The foliage parted slightly, just enough for me to catch a glimpse of something… someone.

"Marcus Cole." The name escaped my lips before I could reel it back in. I recognized him from the papers from ten years ago. There he was. Standing in the bushes, hiding behind them, looking like a portrait of ruin, his clothes hanging off him in tatters, face gaunt with dark circles underlining his watchful eyes.

"Who are you? I saw you in my bungalow, touching my things."

He breathed out, the words tangled in a mess of disbelief and fear. His emergence from the shadows was like a ghost stepping forth from its haunting, the past bleeding into the present.

"I'm FBI Agent Thomas," I said. "Marcus, why are you here?" I kept my voice level, but inside, my pulse throbbed.

"Why are you asking?"

"Because you being here makes it look like you are here for revenge. Maybe you already had it? Did you kill Mark?"

He shook his head with a snort. "You gotta be kidding me."

"Then help me, Marcus. Tell me why you're here. Why are you hiding in a seemingly empty bungalow?"

"Isn't it obvious?" His laugh was a sharp burst, bitter as the salt tang in the air. "I'm searching for something."

"Searching? Or hiding?" The accusation hung heavy between us like the oppressive humidity of the island.

"Hiding? From what, Agent Thomas?" His gaze darted left, then right, like a caged animal seeking an escape. "The ghosts of my past?"

"Mark's dead, Marcus. You're linked to him, to Isla. Can't ignore that."

"Linked by lies!" His fist clenched and unclenched, a rhythm of frustration. "You think this is easy? Being back here?"

"Easy? No. But necessary? Maybe." I stepped closer, watching the muscles in his jaw twitch. "Tell me your side of the story."

"Side…," he scoffed, his voice cracking. "Sides imply fairness. There was nothing fair when they locked me up at seventeen!"

"Then help me understand," I urged, trying to pierce his armored exterior.

"Understand?" His eyes blazed, and his hands shook with barely restrained fury. "You can't. Not unless you've been in that hellhole."

"Try me."

"Ten years," he spat out. "Ten years in a cell, while the real killer walked free."

"Who, Marcus? Who's the real killer?"

"Wouldn't you love to know?" His smirk was quick and vanished fast, leaving behind a shadow of pain. "Like anyone would believe me now."

"Try me," I repeated, softer this time.

"Believe a convict?" He shook his head, a lock of hair falling into his eyes. "No one listens to a ghost."

"Marcus, ghosts don't leave footprints. You're alive. Talk."

"Alive?" Bitter laughter again. "You call this living?"

"Better than giving up."

"Who says I've given up?" His stance shifted, a glimmer of his old defiance sparking within him.

"Prove it. Help me solve Mark's murder."

"Help? At what cost, Agent Thomas?" His words were shards of glass, sharp and scattered.

"Justice has no price tag."

"Justice," he mused, the word foreign on his lips. "Is that what we're calling it these days?"

"Call it what you want," I said, holding his gaze. "But if you know something—"

"Knowing isn't enough." His shoulders slumped just for a moment, revealing the burden he carried. "It never was."

"Doesn't mean you shouldn't speak out."

"Speak out?" He snorted. "To who? The same people who didn't listen before?"

"Things have changed, Marcus. I'm listening."

"Are you?" Suspicion laced his question. "Or are you just waiting to slap cuffs on me again?"

"Only if you're guilty."

"Guilty...." He trailed off, lost in memories only he could see. "Was guilty before I even spoke a word. Remember?"

"The past doesn't have to be prologue, Marcus. We can write a new chapter here."

"New chapter, huh?" He looked at me then, really looked, and I saw a flicker of hope in the ruin. "Maybe...."

"Start talking."

"Talking leads to trouble."

"Silence breeds it."

He weighed my words, the internal battle playing across his face. Finally, with a deep breath that seemed to dredge up the very depths of his soul, he took a step forward.

"Fine. But if I talk, you've got to promise—"

"Anything."

"Promise me you'll keep an open mind."

"Always do."

"Alright," he said, nodding slowly, a decision made.

"Let's start from the beginning," I said.

"The night Isla was—This guy who is here at the resort now, I've seen him around, was...."

A crackle of leaves underfoot cut through the humid air, slicing our exchange in two. We both froze, instincts flaring like a match struck in darkness. I scanned the thick foliage, my trained eyes searching for the source of the intrusion.

"Did you hear that?" I whispered.

"Footsteps," he breathed out, already edging away.

"Wait, Marcus—"

"I can't." His gaze darted around the clearing, wild and desperate. "Not again."

"Marcus, don't run. I need to know what you mean. What about that guy? Who is he?"

"I need to go."

"No, Marcus. You don't have to be afraid."

"Easy for you to say," he spat back, "with your badge and your backup."

"Backup is miles away. It's just us here. Cut off from the world."

"Exactly," he said, as the footsteps grew louder and closer. "I need to make sure no one knows I'm here."

"Whatever happens, I can protect you," I urged, but the panic had taken hold, churning through him like a current.

"Sorry, no can do." He backed into the shadows, a ghost of a man wronged by life one too many times.

"Marcus, damn it!" My frustration boiled over as he vanished into the greenery, each rustling leaf marking his retreat.

I paced the clearing, my thoughts a whirlwind. Marcus's taut face, his insistent claims—they clung to me like burrs. Could the truth be so twisted? Ten years had passed since Isla's case closed; ten years of rotting lies? What did he mean to say about this guy? Who was he?

I looked around but found no one, then I hurried back to my bungalow. There on the wooden porch, I saw something.

My heart hitched.

I crouched, hands parting leaves with surgical precision. There, nestled as if by an afterthought, lay an unmarked envelope—ivory against the green tapestry.

Fingers trembling, I broke the seal. The note inside unfolded with a soft crease, the letters stark against the white paper:

"Stop looking, or you'll be next."

No signature, no flourish, just those words like ice water down my spine.

"Great," I murmured, scanning the untamed brush around me as if the trees held prying eyes. My pulse hammered, each beat echoing the threat scrawled in block letters.

"Threats now? Really?" I scoffed into the void, but the bravado couldn't mask the dread seeping into my bones.

"Whoever you are, better watch your back," I whispered, a silent promise to the wind. My jaw set, my gaze hardened. I had to shield Olivia, even if it meant walking through fire.

"Game on," I breathed, stepping forward with newfound determination. The stakes were clear, and I was all in.

Chapter 22

THEN:

The security guard's grip was unyielding; his hands clamped around Javier's arms like iron bands as he escorted him toward the boat that would take him away from the island, never to return. With each step he took away from Isla, the tightness in his chest grew, a physical manifestation of the heartache that threatened to consume him. Yet, even in this moment of anguish, Javier's gaze never wavered from Isla's. His eyes, bright with unshed tears, held a silent promise —a vow that not even the steely force of Victoria's will could smother the flames of their love.

Isla stood motionless, her feet rooted in the sand that had been their sanctuary mere moments ago. The world tilted on its axis, her senses numbed by the spectacle unfolding before her. The vibrant colors of the beach faded into a monochrome palette, the laughter and warmth sucked out of the air, leaving a void that echoed with Javier's absence. The sharp scent of saltwater stung her nostrils, a cruel reminder of the distance growing between them with every heart-wrenching second.

As the security guard's silhouette dwindled, merging with the seafoam green of the estate's manicured hedges, Javier turned for one last look. His dark, curly hair whipped about his face in an untamed dance. Even from afar, the resilience etched into Javier's features was unmistakable—his spirit might be bruised, but it remained unbroken.

"Javier!"

Isla's voice cracked. She raised a trembling hand, reaching out to the space her love had occupied, now filled with nothing but the ghosts of their shared dreams.

With Javier's departure, the beach transformed into a desolate landscape, its beauty marred by the jagged edge of loss. Isla's knees buckled, and she crumpled to the ground, her fingers digging into the sand as if trying to hold onto something tangible in the chaos.

Tears blurred Isla's vision, the cascading waves of the ocean merging with the stream of her grief. She wrapped her arms around herself, holding on to the fading heat of Javier's touch, a feeble shield against the chill of abandonment. And there, in the shadow of the home that was no longer a sanctuary, Isla let the waves of sorrow crash over her, alone yet resolute in the knowledge that this was not the end.

The waves whispered to Isla, their rhythmic lapping against the shore a soft murmur beneath her sobs. She rose slowly, her legs heavy as if weighed down by the gravity of her mother's verdict. Standing alone on the sand, she could feel the remnants of the day's heat fading away with the retreating sun, leaving a cool film on her sun-kissed skin.

Isla's gaze lingered on the horizon, where the sea met the sky in an indistinct line—much like the blurred boundaries between love and duty that seemed to suffocate her now. The ocean, once a symbol of uncharted freedoms and shared secrets with Javier, now stretched out before her like an expanse of uncertainty. The salt in the air clung to her lips, a bitter reminder of tears shed and words left unsaid.

Her mother's wrath hung over her like the gathering dusk, its weight settling in her chest and constricting her breath. With her cold determination and stony heart, Victoria Walton had spoken words that cleaved through Isla's dreams, severing them from the possible futures they might have woven together.

Yet, even as the tide pulled at the shore, eroding it grain by grain, so too did a resolve begin to form within Isla's spirit. Her mother's disapproval, fierce as it was, could not drown out the steady drumbeat of her own heart—a heart that beat for Javier, for the promises they had vowed to keep.

She took a deep, shuddering breath, tasting the salty air mixed with her resolve. The ocean's vastness mirrored the depth of her inner struggle, the waves reflecting the tumultuous emotions that crashed within her. Isla knew if she was ever to see Javier again, it would be through clandestine meetings and whispered defiance. It would be dangerous, and she could lose everything.

Was it a risk she was willing to take?

As darkness fell, Isla remained steadfast, a solitary figure framed against the twilight. She cast a final glance back at the house that loomed behind her, its windows dark and unwelcoming. Then, turning her face toward the ocean, she let the fading light wash over her. The lingering sense of tension and anticipation was palpable, a silent promise to herself and Javier that no matter what was to come, she would navigate it.

For Javier. For love.

Chapter 23

I WEAVED THROUGH THE RESORT, my eyes locked on Clementine. The housemaid's hands fluttered over polished silver-ware. I caught her in the alcove, away from the crowd.

"Clementine," my voice was a hushed blade, "what do you know about Emilio's ties to this island?"

She stiffened, the gleam of the chandelier above us reflecting off her wide eyes—a silent beat, then another, each one thudding against my chest like an accusation. My gut churned; something wasn't right. I had been thinking about the man Marcus mentioned and thought of Emilio. He knew Isla back then, he said. Was that the guy Marcus was talking about?

"Ms. Thomas," she breathed, barely audible. "Not here."

"Then where?" I pressed, urgency sharpening my words.

"Walk with me." She glanced around, shoulders tense, eyes sharp darts seeking eavesdroppers.

We slipped into the rhythmic flow of servants invisibly attending to the guests' every whim. Her whisper broke the cadence, "Emilio... he's hiding more than anyone knows."

"More?" The word escaped me, heavy with implications. "What do you mean?"

"Much more." Her lips barely moved. "Dangerous truths."

Every muscle in my body coiled, ready to spring into action. This—this was why I needed to speak to Emilio. Every instinct as an agent, every ounce of protective drive as a mother, screamed for resolution.

"Can you—?" I started.

"Shh." A finger to her lips, her gaze a signal flare of caution. We'd talk more. Later. For now, Clementine's words clung to me, a second skin of suspicion. What was it about this man, this Emilio? I needed answers. I would get them.

Guests strolled around the shimmering pool. They chatted quietly among themselves, their voices a gentle hum mingling with the faint sound of splashing water. Some gathered in small clusters, their heads bowed together as if sharing secrets. They were probably concocting elaborate stories about how my daughter, with her serene smile and poised demeanor, could have possibly turned out to be a murderer and how she killed her best friend in cold blood. The air was thick with speculative whispers as each guest contributed their own version of events to the narrative.

Ugh.

I watched Emilio from the corner of my eye, his mysterious presence drawing me in.

"Time to move," I muttered under my breath.

Palm trees swayed as if they were privy to my plan, whispering secrets to the ocean breeze.

"Ms. Thomas, to what do I owe the pleasure?" Emilio's voice was a velvet trap as I approached him.

"It's not really the place or time for small talk, is it?" I said smoothly, sidling up beside him. "Care for a walk?"

His eyes narrowed, sensing the undertone in my invitation. "Is there something on your mind?"

Gravel crunched under our feet, breaking the silence as we ventured farther from the main house. A secluded grove of palms lay ahead. We stopped, and the only sound was the rustle of leaves in the wind.

"Here's good," I said, my voice low.

Emilio's arms wrapped around himself, a barrier against vulnerability. "What's this about?"

"Your secret," I began. "You were here on the island when Isla died, weren't you?"

His eyes darted away, then back, fierce. "Who told you?"

"Doesn't matter. I need to know more," I pressed.

"Why? Why should I trust you?" He was a statue.

"Because I'm here to help." My tone softened. "I want to understand."

"Understand?" He scoffed, but his rigid stance faltered. "You have no idea."

"Then explain it to me," I urged. "Please."

He exhaled sharply, a fortress considering its gates. "It's… complicated."

"Most truths are." I edged closer, my words a gentle prod. "Start somewhere—anywhere."

Emilio looked out to the ocean. "Fine," he relented, "but this goes deeper than you can imagine."

Chapter 24

EMILIO'S GAZE fixed on a point somewhere in the distance, his voice barely above a whisper.

"Isla and I, we were... it was like we breathed each other's souls."

"Souls," I echoed, my own breath catching at the rawness in his tone. "That's deep. And very poetic. You loved each other?"

"Her laughter was my heartbeat." A sad smile touched his lips for a fleeting moment before despair reclaimed its territory. "And then it stopped."

"Because of her family?" My question sliced through the quiet evening air, sharp and direct.

"Her mother," Emilio corrected, spitting out the words as if they were poison. "She couldn't stomach us—our love. My real name is Javier. I used a different name when I came here, so Mrs. Walton wouldn't know it was me who was coming with her sister. Beatrice told me to do that. Otherwise, I wouldn't have been invited. Beatrice told Victoria that she wanted her friend to be with her.

"Why?"

"I don't know. Beatrice contacted me a couple of weeks ago and asked me to attend Mark's party. At first, I said there was no way I was ever going back there, but she told me it was important and that I should do it for Isla. Beatrice was the only one who helped us back then, who thought it was okay for us to love one another. So, I trusted her and came with her. When Victoria saw me, she almost lost it, but she couldn't do anything about it since all the guests were already here. I still don't know why Beatrice wanted me to come. But seeing Mark... dead the same way Isla died, it... it almost broke me."

"Tell me what happened back then," I urged, though every word seemed to carve deeper into his torment.

"Her mother found out about us. It was awful. The screaming, the threats...." His fingers twisted together, knuckles white. "It was relentless, suffocating."

"Did she threaten Isla?"

"Us both." Emilio's voice cracked, and he paused to swallow hard. "But Isla bore the worst of it. She was trapped by the family's expectations."

"And that led to...."

"I was thrown off the island. My mother continued to work and stay here for at least a few years before she left. I lost everything that day. I grew up here on this island. It was also my home."

"What about your father?" I asked.

"He left when I was young. Mrs. Walton took in my mother and me and made sure my mom had a good job. She was always so good to us. Until... until."

"You fell in love with her daughter."

"Yes. It ruined everything. She had me escorted off the island and told me never to return. I was eighteen."

"And then what happened?"

"Then, a few days later, Marcus killed Isla. It was the most awful thing in the world."

"And who was Marcus Cole to her again?" I asked. "If you were the love of her life?"

"He was her cover, her boyfriend that her mother wanted her to be with instead of me. I suppose he became jealous upon learning about her love for me. No one really knows exactly what went on that night."

"So, you weren't there? You weren't on the island?"

"No. I was staying with my uncle and his wife in Marathon Key. I heard what had happened from her Aunt Beatrice, who called me the next day and told me. A big part of me died with her that day. And even though I loved her the most, I wasn't even allowed to go to the funeral. Her mother wouldn't let me. Marcus confessed to the murder the day after she was found, and that was it. I eventually moved on with my life. But I never forgot about her."

My heart clenched as the pieces fell into place, the tragic mosaic of Emilio's past revealing itself.

"Thank you, Eva Rae," he whispered, his voice steadier than before. "For believing me."

"Thank you for sharing." My reply was simple, but it carried the weight of my resolve.

I spun on my heel, gravel crunching underfoot, as I marched back to the main house. Each step punctuated my thoughts—sharp, clear, determined.

"Think, Eva, think," I muttered, replaying Emilio's revelations in my head. The pieces were there, scattered, waiting for me to fit them together.

My mind scrolled through guest profiles, alibis, and timelines. Patterns emerged, a sinister tapestry weaving through Paradise Key's idyllic façade. I needed angles, leverage, something to pry open the tight-lipped secrets this place harbored.

"Hello, main house," I greeted the imposing structure as it came into view, its windows like watching eyes.

"Let's see what ghosts you're hiding," I said, more to myself than anyone who might overhear. "Time to shake things up," I promised myself as I stepped onto the veranda.

Chapter 25

I RESTED against the old wooden veranda railing, my eyes locked on the horizon where dark clouds churned like turbulent thoughts. The wind, signaling an approaching thunderstorm, rustled the palm trees into a flurry of whispers.

The main house welcomed me back as I stepped inside. Guests had gathered, waiting for lunch, some already clutching drinks to quell the unease we all felt but couldn't shake. I greeted my friends, Michelle and Jen, who were deep in conversation until I joined them.

"Ladies," I nodded. "Seems like a storm is brewing out there." They both smiled, nodding awkwardly, and I decided to let them continue their hushed discussion.

I picked up a plate to get some shrimp when I heard footsteps behind me. Not the soft kind, but deliberate and purposeful. I straightened, my instincts sharpened by years in the field. I turned to see her—the ice queen in all her splendor.

"Beatrice," I said, keeping my tone steady, my eyes narrowing slightly as I assessed her. I had hoped to encounter her here. "What can I do for you?"

"Let's skip the niceties, Eva Rae. We both know this isn't a friendly visit." Her voice cut through the room with the precision of her well-tailored suit.

"Then let's dive in." My response was brief, ready for the verbal duel to commence.

"Your investigation," Beatrice started, her steely gray eyes fixing on mine, "has it uncovered anything about Victoria?"

"Should it have?" I countered, leaning back against the table.

"Stop playing games with me, Eva Rae." She stepped closer, her voice lowering to a sharp whisper. "You and I both know that woman holds secrets darker than those black clouds approaching."

"That's your sister. It seems a little harsh. Claims like that need proof, Beatrice." I held her gaze, refusing to waver under her intense scrutiny.

"Perhaps," she said, her lips curling slightly, "but intuition often leads where evidence eventually follows."

"Sure," I said, getting tired of her games. Beatrice was definitely playing her own agenda right now and had been ever since deciding to bring Emilio or Javier here to upset her sister. But why? What was she up to?

"You need to look closer at Victoria," Beatrice continued, her tone sharp. "Mark's mother has a history of her own—a lover."

I could see the threads of her words weaving a complex story, hinting at secrets buried deep within the very fabric of Mark's family history.

"Hm…," I said, letting it hang in the air between us. "You seem quite invested in Mark's death, Beatrice. Is there a personal stake in all of this?"

Her expression remained impassive, but I caught a flicker of something fleeting in her eyes before it vanished behind a mask of icy control.

"I have my reasons," Beatrice replied cryptically, her gaze piercing through me. "I'm also his aunt."

Before I could probe further, a sudden crash of thunder reverberated through the house, followed by a blinding flash of lightning that illuminated the room in stark relief.

"We'll continue this later," Beatrice stated with finality, turning to leave as the lights flickered momentarily, casting eerie shadows across the room. I watched her depart, her figure disappearing into the dimly lit hallway as the storm unleashed its fury outside. The tension in the air lingered long after she had gone.

Chapter 26

Isla Montgomery sat at the kitchen table, the morning light bathing the room in a soft glow. Her fingers danced across the wood grain, tracing patterns as labyrinthine as her thoughts. The confrontation with her mother had left her reeling—a whirlwind of anger, sorrow, and defiance swirling in her chest. Yet as she breathed in the scent of brewing coffee, Isla's resolve hardened like the aged oak beneath her fingertips. Today, like every day, she would wear her composure like armor.

The sound of footsteps heralded a shift in the air, a drop in temperature that had nothing to do with the season. Victoria Walton entered, her silhouette framed by the doorway, each step a study in controlled elegance. The ice-blue eyes that flicked toward Isla carried the chill of winter, and her voice, when it came, was the sharp edge of frost.

"Darling, must we go through this every morning?" There was a smile on Victoria's lips, but it never reached her eyes. "That hair of yours—it looks as though you've been caught in a gale. And those clothes... They might be suitable for a bohemian escapade but not for a lady of your standing."

Isla kept her gaze steady, even as she felt the sting of the barb. She was well aware of the game of appearances her mother played, the subtle warfare waged with words and looks.

"Mother, the wind has a mind of its own," Isla replied, her voice even, betraying none of the turmoil churning within her. She tucked a rogue strand of hair behind her ear and smoothed the front of her blouse with a practiced hand. "And as for my clothes, I find comfort in simplicity."

The clothes, the hair—it was all a protest against her mother and what she had done to Javier, and they both knew it.

Victoria arched an impeccably shaped eyebrow, her lips thinning momentarily before she pivoted on her heel, dismissing the conversation and Isla entirely.

With a sigh that carried the weight of years, Isla pushed back from the kitchen table and escaped into the refuge of the garden. The air was fresh here, untainted by the stifling expectations that filled the house. She walked past the hedges, trimmed with geometric precision, and found solace in the wild beauty of the flowerbeds, where Clementine knelt, her hands deep in the rich soil. Usually, Clementine would take care of the household inside, but she had such a passion for flowerbeds that Victoria had allowed her to tend to some of them, and it had become her sanctuary, her place of freedom. Clementine had been with them ever since Isla could remember, and sometimes she was more of a mother to her than her own mother.

"Those roses will bloom beautifully, Clem," Isla said, her voice softer now.

Clementine looked up, a smile creasing her weathered face. "They're resilient, much like you, dear," she said, brushing dirt from her hands. "What's troubling you?"

Isla took a seat on the stone bench nearby, watching a butterfly flit from blossom to blossom.

"It's Mother. She expects me to be someone I'm not—and I fear I'll drown in the life she's crafted for me."

"Your spirit is strong, Isla," Clementine reassured her. "You are your own person, no matter what anyone else wishes of you."

Clementine's hands paused mid-air, a tender lavender sprig held delicately between her fingers.

"Sometimes," Clementine began, her voice as soft as the breeze that rustled through the greenery, "we must prune away the parts of our lives that no longer serve us, even though they've been with us for so long." She placed the sprig in her basket and turned her full attention to Isla, her gaze warm and knowing.

Isla let out a breath she hadn't realized she'd been holding, comforted by the presence of the woman who had always been a pillar of silent strength in the chaotic world of the Walton household. "But how do I begin, Clem? Where do I find the courage?"

"Courage isn't something you find, dear. It's something you build, day by day—like these flowers. You nurture it, care for it, until one day it blooms inside you, strong and beautiful." Clementine reached out to tuck a stray lock of hair behind Isla's ear, a maternal touch that spoke volumes.

As Clementine returned to her work, Isla watched her with a mix of admiration and wistfulness. The quiet of the garden seeped into her bones, and with it came an unfamiliar sense of clarity. She traced the lines of her own palms, seeing them not just as part of herself but as instruments of her fate.

Could she truly carve out a path different from the one her mother had so meticulously planned? The thought was like a seedling pushing through hard soil—fraught with difficulty, yet undeniable in its existence. Her heart ached with longing for the freedom to express the love she harbored for Javier and to embrace the unpredictable beauty of life beyond these walls.

"Maybe it's time," Isla whispered to herself, her voice barely audible over the chirping of crickets. "Time to cultivate my own garden."

Chapter 27

I SNATCHED my phone from the cluttered desk, my fingers fumbling with the screen until Matt's name lit up. I returned to the bungalow, wanting to check in on them at home. The wind howled against the sides of the small cabin. As the call connected, I steadied my breathing, bracing for his voice.

"Hey, it's me," I said.

"Everything okay?" His words came through crisp, the calm in his voice soothing me.

"Quick check-in. How are the kids?"

"Safe, sound, and submerged in pizza," he chuckled. "Alex tried to build a pizza tower, but Angel kept swiping the pepperoni off the top."

I laughed softly, imagining their antics. "That sounds like them. Remember last week when Angel insisted her teddy bear could play hide and seek better than anyone else?"

"Oh, yes," Matt said with a grin in his voice. "And Alex was so determined to prove her wrong that he ended up under the bed, claiming victory when no one could find him."

"That was fun," I murmured, swallowing the lump that had

formed in my throat. I missed them all so, so much. "Matt, this is… it's a lot."

"Talk to me, Eva Rae. What's going on?"

"Later," I promised, my gaze drifting to the darkening sky outside. "Just wanted to hear your voice and know that things are okay at home."

"All is well. Be careful," he said, soft yet firm.

"Always am." I ended the call, my resolve hardening like the tropical timber walls surrounding me. I went to Olivia's room and knocked, then opened the door. She wasn't there.

"Olivia?"

"In the bathroom," she yelled from behind the closed door.

The room was a mess. I walked inside, picked up her shorts from the floor, folded them, and put them on the bed.

The room felt smaller as I turned toward Olivia's belongings, which were scattered across all the furniture.

"What a mess," I mumbled, and I started to pick up pieces of clothing. "I can't believe this."

And then—there it was. Tucked beneath a stack of beachwear, I found a white T-shirt. I lifted it up in the light, then gasped. There was a big crimson stain across the white cotton. My pulse hammered, echoing the thunder that shook the foundations of the bungalow.

"Jesus," I breathed, seizing the T-shirt, the bloodstain stark and accusing. I scanned the room, half-expecting a natural explanation to present itself. None did.

Olivia came out of the bathroom. Our eyes met as she stood in the doorway, staring first at me, then at the shirt between my hands.

"Olivia!" The name sliced through the humid air, each syllable heavy with accusation and dread. I thrust the T-shirt forward like a flag of war, its stain a grotesque painting.

"Explain this—now!"

Her eyes, those pools reflecting our shared stubborn streak, widened in shock. Her hands fluttered to her mouth, her fingers trembling. Images of the cut on Mark's hand flashed before my eyes.

Was this Mark's blood?

"Mom, I—I don't—" she started, her voice faltering.

"Blood, Olivia." My words were steel, clipped, and cold. "Whose is it?"

"I don't know," Olivia stammered, her composure fracturing. Tears shimmered on the brink of spilling over; her denial felt weak against the roar of the wind that battered the bungalow.

"I don't buy that for a minute! This isn't just some teenage mess you can sweep under the rug," I pressed, the urgency pricking my skin. "This is very serious."

"Mom, please," she pleaded, her breath hitching. "It's not—"

"It's not what I think? Then what is it?" My voice rose, adamant. "Where did this blood come from?"

"Nothing happened!" Her words were nearly lost, a whisper swallowed by the building tempest. She looked away, a portrait of torment against the backdrop of an angry sky.

"Olivia, look at me!" I demanded, reaching for her, desperate to wrench the truth from her quivering lips. But the wind howled louder as if nature itself was conspiring to keep her secrets safe.

"Stop it!" Olivia's voice cracked like the whip of lightning outside, her hands darting out to seize the bloody evidence from my grip. The T-shirt hung between us for a suspended second before she wrenched it free.

"Olivia—" I began, but she was already moving.

"Stop!" she hurled back at me, her voice laced with raw emotion. Her feet drummed a rapid retreat across the wooden floor, each step a loud noise in the otherwise silent bungalow.

"Olivia!" My call was stern and authoritative, but she didn't slow. She slammed the door open, and the wind snatched it from her grasp with a violent thud against the wall.

I stood there, the space where the T-shirt had been still warm in my hands. With a deep breath, I followed, reaching the doorway just in time to see her figure blur into the storm's fury.

"Olivia!" I shouted, but the wind swallowed my words whole.

She ran away, her silhouette etched briefly as lightning forked across the sky. Thunder growled a warning, rolling over the island like an angry beast awakened.

When the electric light caught her face, it was a canvas of despair and defiance, tears carving clean lines down her cheeks. She didn't look back; her body was angled forward against the gale that now whipped her hair into wild tendrils.

"Damn it," I muttered, heart racing with the same intensity as the heavens above. I knew better than to let her go alone into this. I knew the danger wasn't just the storm itself but what brewed within her, untamed and desperate.

"Olivia!" My voice fought to rise above the cacophony of nature's rage, hoping beyond hope that it would reach her, that it might get her back to safety, back to me.

But she was gone, devoured by the storm, leaving only the echo of her flight and the unanswered questions that howled with the wind.

I went after her.

Of course, I did.

Chapter 28

"OLIVIA!"

My plea was a mere whisper against the wind's howl. I stumbled forward, the first sheets of rain pelting me like shards of glass.

"Olivia!" This time, with more force and determination steeling my voice despite the wind's insistence on silencing me. My feet skidded on the slick wooden planks of the bungalow's porch as I launched myself forward.

Rain hammered down, stinging my eyes and blurring my vision. I blinked rapidly, striving to keep sight of the retreating figure that had been my daughter only moments before. The world around me had become a watercolor painting left out in the rain, edges bleeding, forms melding together under the onslaught.

"Olivia, stop!" I gasped, my breath catching in my throat as gusts of wind fought my advance. Palm trees bowed and danced in a frenzied tango above me, unsettled by the encroaching fury of nature.

"Mom, go back!" Her distant cry reached me, distorted and fragmented. But it was her voice, unmistakably Olivia's.

"Can't do that!" I yelled back, though I wasn't sure she heard. My agent instincts kicked in, every sense attuned to the chaos, searching for order within it. I had to reach her, had to bring her back from the brink—whatever it took.

Lightning cleaved the sky, a brief, brilliant guide lighting my path. Thunder boomed, an unrelenting drumbeat urging me on. The rain turned torrential, a relentless downpour that soaked through my clothes. Yet, my heart burned with worry, pounding a rhythm that matched the heavens.

I couldn't see her anymore.

"Olivia!"

No response. Only the sound of the wind, mocking and challenging.

"Damn," I gritted out between clenched teeth, pushing onward. Ahead, the foliage whipped into a frenzy, thrashing as if to block my way. Each step was heavier and slower as I fought the deluge that sought to drive me back.

"Come on, Eva," I muttered to myself. "Keep moving."

With each blink, the scene before me washed out and snapped back into focus. I was close—I could feel it in my bones, an inexplicable pull toward where she had to be.

"Olivia!" One last effort, one final push. And then, there it was —a fleeting shadow darting into the dense thicket.

"Got you," I whispered to no one, to the wind, to Olivia. With a renewed burst of energy, I plunged after the shadow.

Olivia's silhouette flickered through the palm trees like a ghost. She ran as if chased by the very storm that raged around her, anger and despair fueling each step.

"Olivia!" My voice was growing hoarse, shredded by the wind that whipped around me. Desperation lent volume to my call, cutting through the sound of the howling wind.

She didn't slow, didn't turn. Her secrets, the ones I was so close to unraveling, propelled her deeper into the maelstrom that swallowed the island.

"Stop!" I demanded of the gale, of her, of everything between us.

The ground slipped beneath me—slick, treacherous. I went down hard, a jolt of pain shooting through my palm as it slapped the wet earth—no time for pain. I scrambled up, adrenaline dulling the ache, my gaze locked on the blur of Olivia's retreating back.

"Olivia Thomas, halt!" The federal agent in me cut loose, authority unyielding. It was a demand, not a plea, and it echoed across the distance.

No reply but the mocking howl of the wind, the symphony of thunder and crashing waves.

"Damn it, Olivia, talk to me!"

Nothing.

I surged forward, feet finding purchase where none seemed to exist. The world was reduced to flashes of lightning, the drum of rain, and Olivia's fleeing form. My daughter was out there, alone, afraid, and burdened by truths too heavy for her young shoulders.

Chapter 29

THEN:

Isla sat cross-legged on her bed, the soft hum of the ceiling fan mingling with the distant call of seagulls outside her window. Around her, half-unpacked suitcases lay open like clamshells, their contents a disheveled mix of summer clothes and uncertainty. Her fingers, bronzed from days spent under the coastal sun, moved absentmindedly over the smooth surface of a seashell. Its spirals felt cool against her skin.

This was always her favorite part of summer: when Aunt Beatrice arrived.

Aunt Beatrice had no children of her own and had always been there for Isla when she needed it. This summer, in particular, she needed her more than ever after all that was happening with her mother. No one knew how to handle Isla's mother like Aunt Beatrice. As she helped her unpack, Isla already felt better. Aunt Beatrice's presence immediately washed over her like a gentle wave.

Aunt Bea's smile was a quiet harbor. It was soft, knowing— reaching her eyes that peered out from behind stylish glasses, lenses that seemed to magnify not just the words of a book but the unspoken language of the heart. Those eyes had seen Isla grow, had witnessed every high and low of her life, and now they rested upon her with an empathy that required no translation.

The faintest of lines around Bea's eyes deepened as her smile broadened, a silent testament to years of joy and sorrow shared within the fabric of their family. It was a look that spoke volumes, a wordless acknowledgment that said, "I see you, dear child, and all will be well." With Aunt Bea here, the weight of the unknown felt less daunting, the future less murky.

She was no longer alone.

Isla's gaze lifted from the delicate contours of the seashell to Aunt Bea's familiar face, a surge of gratitude washing over her.

"Aunt Bea," she breathed out, her voice carrying the weight of countless unspoken words. The shell was gently placed on the nightstand as Isla patted the space beside her on the bed, an invitation as much for the company as it was for solace.

"Come sit with me?" she asked, her plea soft yet underscored by a need for the comfort only Bea could provide.

Bea obliged, settling onto the edge of the mattress with a grace that made even this simple act seem like part of a greater dance of reassurance. Her presence was a balm to Isla's frayed nerves, and in the sanctuary of her room, they were just Isla and Bea—family, with no pretenses necessary.

"Can I tell you something?" Isla ventured, her eyes locking onto Bea's with an intensity borne of conflicting emotions.

"Of course, my sweet child," Bea encouraged, her hand finding Isla's, their fingers intertwining. "You can tell me anything. You know that."

Isla took a deep breath, the salt-tinged air of her memories mingling with the faint scent of lavender that always clung to Bea.

"This summer, things have been very difficult," she confessed, her voice a tapestry of hope and fear. "With Mom—Victoria. We've been fighting a lot."

The words hung between them, fraught with the gravity of past grievances and the fragile tendrils of hope. Isla's yearning for reconciliation with her mother was palpable, yet so too was the apprehension that crept into the edges of her tone, painting her desire with shades of uncertainty.

"It's more than usual. Because there's something else," Isla continued, her gaze dropping to where their hands joined. "I've fallen in love with my best friend, Javier, but Mom won't let us be together. She wants me to be with Marcus."

Her eyes sought Bea's once more, searching for reassurance within their depths. Bea squeezed Isla's hand gently, offering a comforting presence.

"Maybe," Bea suggested softly, "you're not giving your mom enough credit. She might understand if you give her the chance. Give it some time. Maybe explain how much you two love one another and then ask her for her blessing."

Isla let out a heavy sigh, torn between the longing for her mother's understanding and the ache of unspoken truths. She knew Bea meant well, but the weight of her past clashes with Victoria clouded her hope for a resolution.

"I don't know if it's that simple," Isla murmured, uncertainty lacing her words as she stared out at the tranquil ocean beyond the resort's boundaries.

Bea's eyes reflected understanding, a glimmer of sadness flashing briefly before she composed herself. "I know it's not easy, my dear," Bea began gently, her voice a soothing balm against Isla's doubts. "But sometimes, the hardest conversations lead to the most healing."

Isla tilted her head, contemplating Bea's words. Her heart was heavy with the fear of confronting her mother's disapproval and disappointment. Yet, beneath the layers of doubt, a flicker of resolve sparked within her.

"You really think she might come around?" Isla said with newfound determination, a hint of steel entering her tone as she met Bea's gaze, a glimmer of defiance in her eyes.

Bea's expression softened, a tender smile touching her lips. "I believe anything is possible when love is at the heart of it, and your mom understands more than you think," she affirmed, her voice imbued with unwavering faith in Isla's ability to navigate the uncertain waters ahead.

As the sun dipped below the horizon, casting a warm glow over the resort and painting the sky, Isla felt a surge of courage welling up within her. She knew the path ahead would be challenging, fraught with insecurity and potential conflict, but she also understood that staying true to herself was the only way forward.

"I'll do it," Isla declared, conviction ringing clear in her voice as she turned to face the main house where Victoria—and family dinner—soon awaited.

"I'll have that conversation with Mom. I will try to get some time alone with her and tell her I love Javier and want to be with him. I'll plead and beg her if I have to."

"That's my girl."

Bea squeezed Isla's hand once more, her eyes shining with pride and unwavering support. "I'll be right here by your side every step of the way," she promised.

Her voice was soothing, securing Isla in her turbulent emotions. She was so happy to have her there with her. She made her feel safe.

Beatrice rose gracefully from the edge of the bed, her presence a column of serenity in the middle of half-unpacked chaos. She placed a reassuring hand on Isla's shoulder, its weight light but grounding. Her eyes, magnified slightly by the stylish glasses perched on her nose, met Isla's with an intensity that was both gentle and penetrating.

"Trust in yourself, Isla," Beatrice said, her voice a soft caress against the uncertainty that hung in the air. "And in the love you hold dear. It will guide you more truly than any compass."

Isla drew in a deep breath, allowing the truth of Bea's advice to seep into her bones. There was strength in her aunt's conviction, a strength that Isla felt stirring within her own chest. She nodded, a silent vow to carry those words with her as she walked the tightrope of family and love.

"Thank you, Aunt Bea." Isla's voice barely rose above a whisper, but it carried the weight of her burgeoning resolve.

With a final squeeze of Isla's shoulder, Beatrice moved toward the walk-in closet, holding a dress on a hanger. Her silhouette, framed against the light from within, seemed to embody the wisdom of the years she had lived and the kindness she had always given so freely.

"Come, let's finish unpacking and then get something to eat. I'm famished."

Chapter 30

I WENT DOWN to the beach to look for her. Sand blasted against my cheeks, stinging reminders of each second slipping away. The storm was a living thing, its breath hot and heavy as it tried to push me back, away from her. But there she was, standing by the water, staring out toward the sea.

"Olivia!" My voice barely cut through the loud noise of wind and waves.

She stood still, too far away, her silhouette etched against the fury of the waves. I charged forward, my heart pounding in my ears louder than the thunder.

"Mom?" Her voice, a fragile thread, reached me.

"Stay there!" I yelled, pumping my legs harder, each step sinking into the shifting sand.

"Mom!"

I saw her turn then, her body tensed like a deer caught in head-lights. The beach was no place for her, not now, not with the sky screaming and the ocean boiling.

"Olivia!" My call was a command, a plea. "We need to get inside, into safety."

When I finally saw it, her face was a turmoil of relief and fear.

The distance closed between us, and every stride was fueled by raw, maternal need.

"Get back to the house!" I ordered, though my voice wavered with the force of my own emotions. "It's not safe out here."

"Mom, I—" Her words were torn away, lost to the wind.

"Olivia, now!" There was no time for discussion, only action, only survival.

The gap between us shrank to nothing, and I wrapped Olivia in my arms. The thunder's rage became a distant drumbeat against the cocoon of our embrace.

"Mom," she gasped, her breath warm on my neck.

"Here now, it's okay." My words were firm, a lifeline in the chaos.

"Everything's spinning," she murmured, clutching me tighter. "It's out of control, Mom. I don't know what to do."

"Focus on my voice, Liv. Just on my voice." I smoothed her hair, matted by the rain.

She nodded against my chest, her body trembling.

"You have to stop running from me. I'm here to help you. Let's talk. But first, let's get out of this weather."

I peeled back to see her face, scanning for that spark of resilience I knew so well. She nodded.

We turned, side by side, and charged toward the shelter of the resort, leaving footprints that the waves would soon claim. Our race against nature, against time itself, propelled us forward. The wind howled its protest, but we were relentless.

"Keep going!" I shouted over the tempest's fury.

"I'm right behind you," she called back, her voice steady now, steel lacing her words.

We burst through the threshold into the sanctuary of the resort. But even as the door closed to the bungalow, sealing away the wind's violence, I felt the weight of the truth heavy in my heart.

"Mom?"

I turned to Olivia, my resolve a silent vow in the space between us.

"I believe in you. I know you didn't hurt Mark. We'll find the answers, sweetheart. We'll make this right."

Her nod, slight but certain, sealed our pact. The storm outside raged on, and within me, I wondered how on earth I would be able to do this. How would I prove my daughter's innocence when everything pointed to her being guilty?

Chapter 31

THEN:

"Marcus, might I steal you away for a moment?" Victoria's voice was soft yet carried an undertone that brooked no refusal. It was just before dinner in the main house when Marcus had gone outside for a breath of fresh air. Isla was still helping her aunt unpack, and he was eagerly waiting for her. She was different somehow than she had been before the summer when they had met up for Easter in the Hamptons, and it worried him. She had spent the first few weeks with Javier, her best friend, and he could see the affection glowing in her eyes as she spoke about him and the fun they'd had. Marcus was no fool and could sense that something was going on.

Victoria gestured toward a narrow path leading away from the main house, its white stone facade glinting in the late afternoon sun.

Marcus nodded, his gaze briefly meeting hers before scanning the expanse of the ocean behind her.

"Of course, Mrs. Walton. Lead the way," he said, his voice a deep rumble.

The path to the cliffside was framed by wildflowers and tall grasses that swayed in the ocean breeze. The sound of waves crashing against jagged rocks grew louder with each step they took, promising privacy that the estate's manicured lawns could not.

Victoria began without preamble as they walked side by side, her eyes fixed on the horizon.

"What's going on, Mrs. Walton?"

"Isla is at a crossroads," she said, her tone even as if discussing something as trivial as the weather. "She needs the kind of stability only certain… traditions can offer."

Her words floated over the sound of the surf, a melody that sought to soothe, though Marcus knew better than to be lulled. He felt the undercurrents of her intentions, as familiar to him as the signs of an impending squall.

"There are certain things in life. Let's call them… tradition. Tradition anchors us," Victoria continued, her hands clasped behind her back. "It gives us a sense of belonging and order."

The breeze caught strands of her hair, whipping them around her face like golden tendrils, but she seemed unfazed, her focus unbroken.

Marcus stepped over a gnarled root that snaked across the path, his boots finding purchase on the uneven ground. He kept his gaze directed outward, at the sharp line of the horizon.

"Your dedication to this family has never gone unnoticed, Marcus. Aligning with us… through marriage would be… beneficial."

Each word was measured, plucked from the air like navigational coordinates meant to guide him to a predetermined destination.

Marcus felt the weight of her gaze upon him, seeking to gauge his response. But he offered none. His loyalty lay with Isla, yet he listened with interest. He loved Isla more than anything or anyone.

"Such a union would ensure prosperity, not just for you, but for Isla as well," Victoria continued, her voice carrying a note of persuasion that sought to cloak the steel beneath. "You have been a steadfast element in her life for years. It's only fitting that you should be rewarded."

The word "rewarded" struck him with the subtlety of a squall. It reeked of transactions and deals—negotiations where the heart had no say. Marcus knew the depths to which the Waltons would dive to maintain their stature and how seamlessly they navigated the currents of power and influence.

"She is, after all, in direct line to inherit the entire fortune, my family fortune, that she will one day share with her brother Mark. That's something to consider as well. You would be set for life, Marcus. It has to count for something, especially... given your background."

His silence remained unbroken. The decision she asked of him was significant, his role crucial. Yet the ocean whispered warnings to him, urging caution against the undertow of Victoria's words. Duty and honor were his guiding stars, but they did not blind him to the potential cost of being caught in the Waltons' riptide.

Marcus placed his hands behind his back. "I do love Isla and remain loyal to her," he said, his voice low and resonant. "That has not changed."

"Of course," Victoria replied, her eyes gleaming with a mix of admiration and calculation. "Your loyalty has never been in question."

A gull cried overhead, slicing through the tension as Marcus nodded tersely. "What's best for her is always at the forefront of my mind." His words were carefully chosen stones, creating a path that steered clear of outright acceptance or denial.

Victoria's lips curved into a smile, though it did not reach her eyes. She turned, gesturing toward the expanse of water that shimmered under the dying light. "Imagine it, Marcus. A future where you stand alongside Isla, hand in hand, lords of this island. Your children would run along these very cliffs, heirs to a legacy built on strength and unity."

Marcus's gaze followed her outstretched arm, taking in the rugged beauty of the landscape. The vision she painted was compelling—a tapestry of tradition and security woven with expert craftsmanship. Yet, it felt like an oil painting, remarkable to behold but lacking the true texture of life.

"But I don't know if this is what is best for Isla."

Victoria's expression faltered for a moment before she regained control, her desperation now almost visible.

"Think of the stability you'd provide for Isla. She admires and respects you. You'd be unstoppable together—a beacon of hope and progress for the entire estate."

He glanced at her, aware of the truth in her words, yet also of the unseen shoals that lurked beneath their surface.

"Maybe, but is that enough for her?" Marcus responded, his tone even. "Don't get me wrong; there's nothing I desire more than to marry her one day. But why the rush?"

Marcus turned to face Victoria. He was only a year older than Isla, and they were both still so young that it almost seemed criminal to discuss marriage.

"Rush? There is no rush. Just a mere concern for my daughter's future," she said. "I would like to know that she's in good hands. Taken care of. I'm not talking about marriage right away... but in the near future."

"Victoria," he began, his voice echoing the grave depth of the waters below, "I can't help but wonder. Is this course we're charting truly for Isla's benefit?"

Victoria waved away his concern with dismissive grace, as though swatting at an insignificant gnat.

"Oh, Marcus, don't be fooled by youthful whimsy. Isla's affection for Javier is nothing but the fleeting fancy of a young heart and an infatuation with the forbidden. It will pass, as such things always do."

She stepped closer, her gaze locked onto his. "You, however, are as steadfast as a mother can dream of. You can give her the stability she needs to grow and flourish. She'll learn to love that about you—about the life you'll build together."

Marcus felt the weight of her words like a pull, strong yet somehow intangible. He understood duty, the call of service to something greater than oneself. But there was something else, too—a whisper of doubt that swirled around him.

Was it okay to marry someone who was in love with another

man? Would that life bring him happiness or sorrow? And what about Isla? Would she be happy?

He glanced at Victoria. The setting sun cast a fiery glow on her face, illuminating the determination etched into her features.

"Victoria," Marcus began, his voice low and even, "you speak of stability as if it's the only compass that should guide us. But what of Isla's own course? Her dreams?"

His gaze remained fixed on the horizon, where the ocean met the sky in an endless embrace.

"Don't you think she deserves to navigate her future by her stars, not ours?"

For a moment, Victoria's composure wavered, as though the very cliffs they stood upon trembled beneath her feet. Her eyes, usually so sure and commanding, flickered with something raw and unguarded. It was gone as quickly as it came—like a rogue wave retreating back into the ocean's depths.

"Marcus," she said, her tone cool but tinged with steel, "I need your help with this matter. I fear that if she… if she falls into the wrong hands, things will go terribly wrong for her." She took a step closer, her eyes locking onto his. "If she follows this direction, our family will have no choice but to cut her off completely. You grew up poor, Marcus. You know what it's like to have nothing."

Marcus felt the sting of her words, the truth in them. As of right now, his mother was sick, very ill, her heart failing her. And they couldn't afford her surgery. Marcus was desperate to make enough money to help her.

Victoria knew this. She knew how desperate he was.

He held Victoria's gaze, the silence between them stretching out like the endless ocean before them. A gull cried overhead.

"Think about it, Marcus. Not only money enough to help your mother get her surgery but also to buy her a new house, a better one, instead of that mobile home you grew up in."

Victoria paced a step ahead, her silhouette sharp against the sky's fading light. She stopped abruptly, turning to face him once more as they reached the end of their path.

"Marcus," she said, her voice carrying a note of urgency that cut through the air like a knife. "You must see the sense in what I'm proposing. It's not just about Isla—it's about all of us. My family and yours. We are at a crossroads, and your union with her could steer us toward calmer waters."

She moved closer, her gaze imploring. The setting sun cast a warm glow on her face, highlighting the earnestness etched into her features. "Isla is lost; she needs you, someone who understands her and loves her. Who better than you?"

Marcus nodded once, a slow, deliberate motion.

"I'll think about it," he said.

His words were sparse, but they carried the weight of a solemn vow, echoing the sense of duty that had always steered his life.

"Thank you, Marcus," Victoria replied, her tone softening. There was a subtle shift in her posture, a release of tension as if she'd been holding her breath, waiting for him to accept the burden of her request. "That's all I can ask for."

Chapter 32

I HAD CONVINCED Olivia we needed to go get some food, and she finally agreed to come with me to grab some dinner from the buffet that Clementine had put out.

We stepped into the main house, and the buzz of conversation died like a snuffed candle. The tension hung so thick you could cut it with a knife—no, that's too worn and cozy. It was more like the air turned to glass, fragile and sharp around us.

"Just ignore them. Keep your eyes on the prize, Olivia," I murmured, my words almost a breath as we navigated through the frozen tableau of guests. "Dinner, remember?"

Olivia nodded, her discomfort radiating like heat waves from asphalt. I hated seeing her this way, like a bird clipped of its wings.

"Right," she replied, her voice barely there but edged with steel. "Dinner."

We pushed forward, the silence splintering with every step we took toward the grand dining room. That's when I caught the acid tones slicing across the room—a verbal fight between Beatrice and Victoria.

"You never did understand, did you?" Beatrice spat, her façade of elegance cracking with each syllable.

"Understand? Oh, I understood plenty," Victoria shot back, her voice searing with resentment.

Their words clawed at the air, echoes of old wounds and bitter grievances laid bare.

"Family first, isn't that what you always say?" Victoria's laugh was devoid of humor, a jagged thing that wanted to wound.

"Family," Beatrice scoffed. She stood tall, her spine a rod of iron. "Your actions speak otherwise."

I edged closer, the investigator in me hungry for the unspoken tales between their barbs. My presence went unnoticed, just another shadow amongst many.

"The past is dead, Beatrice. Let it rest," Victoria hissed, her eyes two flints, sparking fury.

"Dead things have a way of resurfacing, sister," Beatrice countered, her tone as cold as an arctic chill.

"Like you. I never could get you to stay away. And now you come here and bring... him with you? The last person I ever want to see again on this island?"

"Enough," Beatrice said with a snort. "This discussion is over."

Victoria's mouth twisted, but she clamped it shut, burying whatever retort threatened to escape.

I edged closer. My ears pricked up as fragments of their heated exchange drifted to me—whispers of disloyalty and clandestine affairs.

"It's been twenty-six years," Victoria spat, "and still you torment me."

"Because twenty-six years ago, you—" Beatrice's voice cut through like a knife, but the rest was muffled by a sudden swell of music from the grand piano across the room.

I leaned in, desperate for more, but Beatrice caught my gaze. Her eyes narrowed for a fraction of a second before she doused the fire in them, replacing it with ice.

"Good evening, Agent Thomas," she said, every syllable crisp as if plated on silver. She turned her back then, signaling the end of their quarrel with a sharp pivot that dismissed me as effectively as it did her sister.

"Beatrice." I stepped forward, my voice low. "Mind telling me what that was about?"

She faced me again, her expression smooth, unreadable. "Oh, just ancient history."

"History has a way of repeating itself." I held her gaze, trying to peel back the layers of her composure.

"Doesn't it just?" A half-smile played on her lips—a masterstroke of deflection.

"Especially on this island," I pressed, hoping to steer her toward disclosure.

"Agent Thomas, you flatter me with your interest," Beatrice replied, her tone laced with a hint of amusement, "but really, it's nothing."

"Nothing doesn't usually spark such... passion." I gestured vaguely in the direction Victoria had disappeared.

"Passion is often wasted on the trivial, don't you think?" She tilted her head, assessing me with those steel-gray eyes.

"Depends on your definition of trivial," I countered.

"Touché." Another smile, this one acknowledging our little game. "But I'm afraid I have to see to our guests now. If you'll excuse me."

"Of course," I acquiesced, watching her glide away, the very picture of grace under pressure.

As she merged with the crowd, a voice in my head whispered, Not so fast, Beatrice. There were secrets buried here; I could feel them pulsing beneath the surface. And I intended to dig them up.

I hovered at the periphery of the room, the clinking of glasses and muted conversations creating a backdrop to my silent surveillance. Beatrice had retreated to an alcove, her back turned, but the tension in her shoulders betrayed her calm exterior. I approached, careful to keep my footsteps light.

"Beatrice," I said, injecting just enough warmth into my voice to seem nonthreatening. "I have a sister of my own, and we can get pretty heated sometimes, too."

She turned, and a semblance of composure snapped back into

place. "Eva Rae, so you understand how families are. Emotions run high."

"Victoria seemed pretty upset."

"Victoria is passionate," she conceded, her lips tight. "It's her nature."

"Or maybe it's what the conversation was about?"

"Speculation isn't becoming of an FBI agent." Her gaze was steady, but her fingers twitched, betraying a frayed edge.

"Sometimes speculation leads to answers." I leaned in slightly, letting silence stretch between us.

"Perhaps." Beatrice's eyes narrowed. "But not today, Agent Thomas. Leave us be, please. We just lost one of our own, and the police don't seem to be doing much to provide us with answers. It's only natural that emotions run high."

"Understood." I stepped back, nodding.

But as I turned, I caught Emilio's eye. He edged closer, his movements deliberate.

"Agent Thomas," Emilio murmured, a knowing look crossing his features. "Beatrice won't say it, but I will."

"Oh?" I kept my voice neutral, but my pulse quickened. "Say what?"

"Victoria once had an affair," Emilio confided, his tone even. "The family was scandalized—still is. It's the real reason Isla was never allowed to be with me—because of her mother's history. The family wouldn't allow it, and Victoria knew this because they wouldn't allow it for her. They wouldn't allow the scandal it would become."

"Scandal, huh? Would it be enough to kill?"

"Who knows?" He shrugged, his eyes dark pools of implication. "But secrets like that have a way of surfacing at the worst times."

"Thanks, Emilio." I nodded, storing away the information.

"A scandal?" I murmured to myself, the word tasting bitter on my tongue. The echoes of Emilio's words hummed in my ears like a swarm of agitated bees. Victoria, with her seemingly impeccable reputation, was now cloaked in the shadows of a clandestine past.

Could that love affair be the skeleton rattling behind closed doors, enough to push her over the edge?

"Family honor," I continued, half-aloud, "can be a noose as much as a badge." My eyes scanned the elegant crowd, roving over faces that held smiles just a fraction too tight. Each one could be a mask, including my old friends Amy, Jen, Michelle, and Kara.

"Mom?" Olivia appeared at my side, her voice thin with concern. "You're pacing."

"Am I?" I hadn't realized my feet betraying the churn of thoughts within. "Just mulling over some details."

I turned back to the room, my gaze resting on Victoria. There she was, a portrait of poise, but the air around her seemed to crackle with latent energy. Was it possible? Had her secret love, once exposed, ignited a firestorm of disgrace so fierce it could drive her to silence Isla forever? Had she done the same to Mark?

"Rage," I whispered, the hint of a theory taking root. "Fear of humiliation driven rage...." My mind raced back to Isla's case files. If Victoria mirrored that same poisonous hate, could it explain the inexplicable?

"Victoria," I said under my breath, fixing the name in my mind like a target. Was she capable of something like that?

I never got to finish the thought.

BAM

The doors suddenly slammed open with a violence that sent a shiver down my spine. Marcus Cole stormed into the room, his presence like a live wire sparking uncontrollable reactions. Fear and confusion spread through the guests faster than wildfire.

"Marcus!" Victoria gasped, an electric jolt in the word itself. Confusion was evident on her face as she screamed. "It's him, it's him. The one who murdered my Isla. And he's got a gun!"

Her words made the room erupt into chaos as everyone reacted simultaneously.

Chairs clattered against the polished floor as bodies lurched backward, creating a sea of panic that I found myself adrift in. The screams bounced off the walls, each echo a hammer strike to my calm. But calm I remained.

"Stay close," I murmured to Olivia, my voice a life raft in the chaos.

My eyes locked onto Marcus, taking in the graying temples and the shadowed eyes that scanned the room with such intensity it could cut glass.

"Easy there," I said quietly as I edged forward, my hand signaling others to give him space. "Let's talk, Marcus."

Chapter 33

MARCUS COLE WAS a statue of desperation in the center of the room, gun clutched in his trembling hand, its metallic surface catching the scant light that seeped through the blinds. The air, thick with tropical humidity, seemed to congeal around us, stifling any movement. Olivia's eyes flickered to mine—a silent plea.

"Mom...." Her voice was a thread, nearly lost in the charged stillness.

"Stay calm," I mouthed back, my heart pounding against the confines of my practical blazer. The subtle smile that usually played on my lips had vanished, replaced by a determined line. My gaze never wavered from her, projecting every ounce of assurance I could muster.

"Nobody moves." Marcus's voice was ragged, serrated with pain and anger. His finger twitched on the trigger.

"Marcus," I said, stepping sideways, inching closer to Olivia under the guise of steadiness. "Talk to me."

"I have nothing to say." His eyes were two dark whirlpools, drowning in his own torment.

"You must have something you need to get off your chest," I

countered softly, willing him to see reason beyond the barrel of his gun. "Why else are you here?"

"Tell that to the years they took from me!" His voice cracked like a whip, and several guests flinched.

"Years you should get back," I offered, easing another step closer to Olivia. "Starting now, with this moment."

"Years...," he repeated, hollow. The gun dipped an inch, then steadied.

"Let me help you, Marcus." My words were a lifeline thrown into turbulent waters. "Trust me."

"Stay where you are!" Marcus's command sliced through the silence, a jagged edge to every syllable. He paced like a caged animal.

I edged forward, hands aloft as if to catch the words that hung heavy between us.

"Marcus," I kept my voice even, a counterbalance to his unraveling. "Let's talk this through."

"Talk?" The word twisted into a snarl as he whipped around, the gun's muzzle a roving spotlight.

"Put the gun down," I coaxed, one cautious step at a time, bridging the gap with each measured breath. "I'm here to listen."

"Listening...."

Skepticism laced his tone, yet he didn't move to stop me.

"Tell me your story," I urged, feeling Olivia's eyes on my back, trusting me to defuse the imminent catastrophe.

"My story...."

A flicker of something softer crossed his hardened features.

"Your truth," I pressed, closer now, close enough to see the strain in his eyes. "Your side of the story. You were betrayed, weren't you?"

"Betrayal," Marcus spat, the word slicing through the silence. "Yes, that's what it was. You want to know why?" His fingers whitened around the gun, a pale echo of his rage.

I nodded once, sharply. My heart pounded in my chest, every beat a silent drum echoing in the tense air. "Yes, tell me."

"They said it was an open-and-shut case." His laugh was hollow, eyes haunted as they fixed on some unseen point in his past. "A kid from the wrong side of the tracks, easy to pin it on."

"Who?" I asked, voice low, stepping a fraction to the right—closer to Olivia so I could protect her should this end badly.

"Doesn't matter!" he barked, then sighed, his shoulders sagging ever so slightly. "They promised me money. Said my mom's surgery… that it would save her. If I said it was me. That I did it, that I killed Isla."

"Your mother…." I let the words hang, a bridge for him to cross.

"She needed surgery," he whispered. "And I… I caved."

"Marcus," I said, softer now but with a steely undercurrent. "Look at me."

He did, and for a split second, I saw the boy he'd been, scared and alone.

"False confessions can be overturned," I told him, my gaze holding his. "Injustice has a way of coming to light."

"It's too late for justice," he muttered, but there was a plea in his eyes. "I lost my youth in that prison."

Marcus's jaw clenched, a visible pulse throbbing at his temple. His finger twitched on the trigger as someone tried to escape but was stopped as he pointed the gun at her.

"Nobody moves," he growled, the threat hanging heavy in the air like Florida humidity.

Heat crept up my spine as I caught Olivia's gaze. Her sneakers squeaked faintly against the polished floor as she edged closer, the gap between us narrowing with each breath I dared to take.

"I was locked away for ten years," Marcus spat, the gun weaving a dangerous arc through the air. "You know what that does to a man?"

"Survival changes you," I said, my voice steady despite the drumbeat of my heart. "But it doesn't define you."

"Define me?" He laughed, hollow and sharp. "They took everything!"

"Then let's get it back," I countered, my stance firm yet open. "Starting with your story."

"Story?" His lips curled into a sneer. "It's a damn tragedy!"

"Let me help write a new chapter," I offered, hoping to reel him back from the edge. "One where you're heard."

"You can't undo time," he shot back, the gun dipping for a moment before he caught himself.

"Maybe not," I conceded. "But we can start by setting the record straight."

"Set it straight?" Marcus echoed, desperation creeping into his voice. "After all this?"

"Truth has a way of outlasting lies," I told him, keeping my words crisp and clear. "Give it a chance."

His breathing turned ragged, the gun's barrel now a quivering compass of uncertainty.

"How do I know you won't betray me, too?"

"Because I'm standing here with you," I said, my resolve unwavering. "And I won't move until we see this through."

The gun quivered in his hand, a metallic bird about to take flight. Guests clung to each other, their breaths held hostage. The room, a gallery of silent sculptures, waited on the precipice of chaos.

"Marcus," I said, my voice a calm breeze over angry waters, "these people, they're not your enemy."

"Enemies...." His eyes flicked across the faces before him, each one a mask of fear. "They don't even know me."

"Let's change that." I took a step forward, each movement deliberate, unthreatening. "Let them see who you really are."

"See me?" He spat the words out like bitter seeds. "As what? A victim?"

"Survivor," I corrected gently. "A man wronged, standing here now seeking justice."

"Justice...." The word seemed to echo in his mind, finding corners of hope long abandoned. "My mother...." His voice cracked. "She needed me."

"And she still does, Marcus," I reminded him. "But it's not just about clearing your name now. It's about living for her, for the future."

"Future?" His laugh was a dry leaf in the wind. "What future?"

"One where this—" I gestured to the gun, "—isn't the last chapter of your story."

He hesitated, the weapon's ominous dance slowing. I watched a battle wage behind his eyes, the scales of fate tilting with every silent second.

"Your story isn't over," I pressed on, my heart pounding Morse code against my ribs. "You can still rewrite it."

"Rewrite...?" Uncertainty flickered across his face, a candle in the wind.

"Marcus, let me help you," I coaxed, my gaze locked onto his. "Don't let this be where your story ends."

"Ends..." he murmured, his grip on the gun loosening ever so slightly. "Maybe...."

"Marcus, now," I urged.

His arm wavered, the gun's muzzle drifting toward the polished floor. The line of his mouth softened, and for a moment, I could see who he used to be—that seventeen-year-old boy, lost.

"Okay," he breathed, almost inaudibly.

Marcus's gaze clung to mine, a silent pact forming in the space between us.

"Tell me who offered you the money if you confessed to killing Isla," I said.

The room's air felt thick and sticky with anticipation as if time itself was holding its breath. His shoulders bent forward, surrender etching into his posture. The gun's sheen dulled as it descended, an inch from my outstretched palm.

"Marcus—" I started.

And then, something shattered within him. A flicker, a spark. His eyes darkened, retreating into the fortress of his resolve. The gun snapped back up, a barrier between us once more.

"It was her mother," he spat, the word like a bullet. "Victoria. She wanted the scandal to go away. She wanted the case closed and asked me to say I did it."

He wheeled around, a blur of motion and turmoil. He shoved past the frozen bodies of guests, their collective gasp a discordant choir to his retreat. The tropical air swallowed him whole as the door slammed shut behind his fleeing form.

"Wait!" My heart lurched, adrenaline surging.

I cursed under my breath, my mind already racing through the next steps. The chase wasn't over; it had just taken an unexpected detour.

Chapter 34

Isla Montgomery leaned on the balcony railing, her gaze fixed on the horizon. The ocean breeze teased strands of her hair, pulling them loose from the careless bun atop her head. She inhaled deeply, the air filling her lungs and attempting to cleanse the emotions that churned within her.

Her fingers gripped the wooden rail, knuckles turning white as she braced herself against the weight of another day spent under her mother's scrutinizing stare. She wondered about Javier. She hadn't heard from him since he was escorted off the island, and part of her wanted to take the boat to the mainland and find him, leaving all this behind. She missed him terribly, and every day dragged along while she wondered where he was and if he was okay.

"Another day," she whispered to herself, the words barely audible above the lull of the waves below. "Just another day."

With a resolve that seemed to solidify with each step, Isla turned her back to the ocean and walked through the sliding doors into the house. The transition was jarring—the open expanse of nature replaced by the claustrophobic luxury of the island home.

The kitchen was awash with the scent of sizzling bacon and freshly brewed coffee. Clementine stood at the stove while Victoria sat at the counter, reading the newspaper, her posture rigid with an elegance that felt out of place in the domesticity of the morning. Her ice-blue eyes did not waver from the paper in her hand, even as Isla entered.

"Good morning, Mother," Isla said, her voice carrying a brightness she didn't feel. She had hoped Aunt Bea would be there, but she was nowhere to be seen. She hated being alone with her mother these days. She felt like she was constantly being judged and found to be inadequate.

"Morning," Victoria responded without lifting her gaze, her tone clipped.

Isla hesitated, feeling the familiar sting of dismissal. She reached for a cup hanging above the coffee maker.

"It looks like it'll be a beautiful day. Maybe we could go for a walk along the shore later?"

"Perhaps," Victoria replied, though the indifference in her voice suggested otherwise. Clementine plated the breakfast with mechanical efficiency, ensuring each strip of bacon lay parallel to the next.

"Actually, I was thinking—"

"Thinking is a dangerous pastime, Isla," Victoria cut in, her back still to her daughter. "Focus on what needs to be done, not on idle whims."

"Right," Isla murmured, chastened.

Aunt Bea had told her that her mother might be able to understand her if she tried talking to her. It didn't feel like it. Isla poured herself some coffee in one of the pristine white cups. She knew better than to press further when it came to her mother; the barriers between them were as unyielding as the walls of the house.

"Breakfast is ready," Clementine announced, setting the table. Isla took her seat, the chair scraping slightly against the tile floor—an abrasive sound in the silent tension of the kitchen.

Isla's mind wandered as they ate, but she remained vigilant, aware that any sign of distraction would be met with a sharp reprimand. Instead, she focused on the warmth of the coffee as it slid down her throat, willing it to ignite some spark of courage within her to face the rest of the day.

Where are you, Javier? Do you miss me as much as I miss you?

Isla's bare feet sank into the cool sand, each step away from the house loosening the tight coils of tension that wound around her chest as she walked to the beach after breakfast.

The beach was deserted, a vast expanse of solitude that welcomed her tumultuous emotions. She breathed deeply, tasting the salty tang of air as the ocean whispered its ceaseless lullaby. Here, amid the rhythmic crash of waves, she found a reprieve from Victoria's coldness.

With every crest and fall of the water, Isla felt her resolve knitting back together, stitch by fragile stitch. This place, this great and untamed stretch of shoreline, had always been her sanctuary against the weight of her mother's expectations. She would find a way to bridge the gulf that had opened between them, she vowed silently to the waves. There had to be a path back to the warmth they once shared, even if it lay obscured by years of misunderstandings and unspoken words.

A seagull's cry pulled Isla's thoughts backward, unraveling the thread of time to a memory drenched in sunlight and laughter. Victoria was there, as she had been years before, her blonde hair billowing like golden sails caught in the breeze. Mother and daughter had built castles in the sand, their creations rising high before the inevitable tide claimed them. Victoria's laughter, a sound as rare and delicate as the shells they collected, rang in young Isla's ears. Her mother's eyes—those piercing ice-blue mirrors—had softened, reflecting the sky above rather than the hardness of the world they faced beyond the dunes.

"Remember, Isla," Victoria had said, her voice carrying over the sound of the crashing waves, "life is much like these castles we build.

It takes patience and care, but in the end, the waves claim all. We must enjoy the beauty while it lasts."

Back then, Isla hadn't understood the melancholy note in her mother's words or the wistful look that had crossed her face. That day, with the sun warming their skin and the future a distant horizon, nothing seemed impossible.

The memory receded as swiftly as it had come, leaving Isla standing at the water's edge, the ghost of her mother's past smile fading. The stark contrast between then and now pressed against her heart, a reminder of what had been lost. But with loss came the desire for restoration, and Isla was not one to let go easily. She would deal with her mother's moods, navigate her complex psyche, and find reconciliation. She had to believe that the bond they once shared had not been completely washed away—that it still waited to be rediscovered somewhere beneath the surface.

Later that same evening, Isla's footsteps carried a resolve as she trod the familiar path back to the island house, the ocean breeze tangling her hair into wilder waves. The sunlight, golden and brazen, seemed to arm her with a sliver of hope as she pushed open the door, stepping from the vast openness of the beach into the cloistered air of the living room.

Victoria sat ensconced in her favorite chair, a book splayed across her lap, her ice-blue eyes skimming the pages with mechanical precision. There was something unnervingly statuesque about her mother's posture, her blonde hair a flawless frame around an expression that divulged nothing.

"Mother," Isla began, her voice a hesitant intruder in the room's silent order. "Can we talk?"

The request hung like a fragile ornament amidst the ticking of the grandfather clock. Victoria closed the book with a soft thud, her gaze rising slowly to meet Isla's—as if considering the worth of the words offered to her.

"Talk?" A frost edged Victoria's tone, belying the calmness of her exterior. "What is there to discuss that hasn't already been dissected under this roof?"

Despite the chill that swept through the room, Isla moved closer, her heart hammering against her ribs.

"I want to understand why you're so angry with me," Isla said, her voice steadier than she felt. "I want to fix what's broken between us."

"Fix?" Victoria echoed, a curl of disdain at the corner of her lips. "You speak as if it's merely a loose thread on a dress, something to be mended with a needle. You brought shame to our family. That is not easily fixed."

Isla's fingers clenched at her sides. The analogy was a barbed reminder of their world of appearances, where everything was stitched together for show, even when the fabric was tearing apart.

"Isn't our relationship worth repairing?" Isla's plea wove itself into the space between them.

"Relationships," Victoria replied, standing up to face her daughter, "are built on respect and obedience. Two qualities you seem to have forgotten."

Isla met her mother's gaze, searching for some sign of the woman who had once held her hand and promised that life was to be cherished. But the warmth was gone, replaced by an icy fortress.

"Your future hangs by a thread, Isla," Victoria said, her voice low, the threat wrapping itself around Isla's throat. "And I will do what I must to ensure that our family's name remains untarnished."

The weight of those words pressed down on Isla. Yet, beneath the pressure, her resolve did not crumble. It was tempered like steel in fire, growing stronger in the face of her mother's cold resolve.

The silence that stretched between Isla and Victoria was abruptly pierced by the soft click of the door and a draft of fresh air. Marcus stepped into the room, his presence like a breath of relief in the stifling tension. He offered a tentative smile, the corners of his mouth lifting in a hopeful curve as he glanced between the two women.

"Seems I've walked into a winter's tale," Marcus joked lightly, attempting to thaw the cold front with his warmth. His eyes flickered with a spark of concern as he searched Isla's face for signs of distress.

But Victoria's expression remained frozen, her lips a flat line that refused to acknowledge the levity.

"Some tales are better left untold," she responded crisply, turning away as if to dismiss the attempt at ease.

Marcus's smile faltered, but he masked the momentary disappointment with a practiced ease, pivoting toward the practicalities of the evening. "Well, dinner awaits, shall we?" he offered, extending the olive branch of normalcy.

The dining table was set with precision, each utensil aligned with obsessive care—an echo of Victoria's control. The clink of silverware against fine china punctuated the strained silence that enveloped them all as they took their seats. Under the chandelier's soft glow, shadows danced across the walls, mirroring the concealed turmoil beneath the surface. Aunt Bea tried to make subtle conversation, but only Marcus engaged with her. Isla stared into her plate, pushing her potatoes around with her fork, while her mother sent her disapproving looks and told her not to play with her food.

Isla willed herself to swallow not only the overcooked lamb but also the emotions and frustration. Each thinly veiled threat that slipped from Victoria's lips sparked anger within her.

"Pass the salt, would you?" Victoria's request sliced through the quiet, her tone casual yet sharp as a scalpel. It wasn't just seasoning she sought, but compliance, a subtle reminder of their hierarchy at the table.

"Of course, Mother," Isla replied, the words tasting of vinegar on her tongue as she handed over the crystal shaker.

"Remember, Isla," Victoria added, her gaze piercing as she sprinkled salt sparingly. "A dish can be spoiled by excess, just as a young woman's prospects can be marred by... indiscretions."

The threat hung heavy in the air, a noxious perfume that threatened to choke Isla. Yet she met her mother's eyes, her own alight with a silent defiance that needed no words. She felt the fabric of her being frayed and worn but not yet torn asunder.

Marcus watched the exchange, his fork paused mid-air. He wanted to speak, to try and make them all feel better, but the unspoken words between mother and daughter held him back. Instead, he focused on his plate.

Aunt Bea set down her utensils, the gentle scrape resonating as though it were a declaration. She cleared her throat.

"Victoria," she began, her voice steady but laced with a firmness that hadn't been there before. "I think what we need is less criticism and more understanding around this table."

Victoria's head snapped up, her eyes narrowing into cold slits. The room seemed to constrict around them, the walls closing in.

"Understanding?" she echoed, the word dripping with disdain. "And what would you know about that?"

"I know enough to see that Isla is trying," she countered. "She deserves compassion, not constant judgment."

The escalation caught Isla off guard. Her heart hammered against her ribs; she couldn't recall the last time anyone had dared to challenge Victoria, let alone in her defense. The air was electric, crackling with the energy of shifting dynamics.

"Compassion?" Victoria scoffed, her voice rising. "It is because I care for her future that I am stern. You wouldn't understand."

"Perhaps," Aunt Bea admitted, her gaze unwavering, "but I understand that support can foster growth better than any amount of fear. You, of all people, should know this. At the very least, talk to her and listen to what she has to say."

Isla felt an unexpected warmth bloom within her chest, a spark of hope. Her mother rose to her feet with a snort of contempt.

"I'm not going to sit here and listen to this. I'm going to lie down. Clementine, I'll take my evening tea in my room."

"As you wish, Mrs. Walton," Clementine said. "As you wish."

Chapter 35

"OLIVIA, NO, STOP!"

My voice was lost in the wind, a useless plea vanishing into the tropical air. I watched helplessly as my daughter's figure disappeared out the door of the resort's main house. Marcus had stormed out seconds before her, a whirlwind of anger and desperation. Olivia yelled that she could stop him, and I was too late to block her way.

Then I heard the shots—crisp and too close—shattering the illusion of paradise.

My heart hammered against my ribcage, each beat spelling out Olivia's name in pure fear. Time slowed to a crawl; the sound of gunfire echoed off the palm trees, drowning the usual serenity of the island in complete chaos.

I sprinted forward past the infinity pool, where once sunbathers lounged in blissful ignorance. Now, it was a chaotic mess of screams. Training kicked in, and my heart rate spiked as adrenaline surged through my veins. The warm breeze that had felt welcoming upon arrival now whipped at my face with unforgiving haste.

"Move!" I barked at a cluster of guests frozen in shock. They scattered, my path clearing as I wove expertly among them. My blazer billowed behind me, an unwanted cape in this real-life horror show.

"Have you seen a teenage girl, short hair, blue T-shirt?" I demanded, grabbing the arm of a staff member who looked like he might faint. The man pointed frantically toward the beachfront bungalows. I didn't waste a breath on thanks, already darting away.

I skirted a toppled trolley of champagne flutes, the shattered glass crunching underfoot. With every turn, every shouted command, I became less of the composed agent and gave in to the primal protectiveness of a mother.

"Olivia!" I called again, voice raw.

The echo of my own desperation rang loud in my ears as I pushed through the manicured hedges that now seemed more like barriers than decorations. Each stride carried me further into the nightmare. More shots were fired. The fearful screams urged me forward.

Please be okay, Olivia. Please. Why would you do that? Why would you run after him?

My breath came in ragged gasps, the humid air sticking to my lungs as I rounded another pavilion. There! A shadow detached itself from the chaos—Marcus Cole. The setting sun cast an ominous glow on his erratic movements, his arm jerking with each shot fired, indiscriminate and wild. Screams punctuated the air like a macabre symphony, guests scattering, their faces masks of fear and disbelief.

"Down! Get down!" I barked at a cluster of petrified staff members huddled by a service entrance, even as I kept moving. My gaze flitted across every corner, every alcove, searching for my daughter.

"Olivia!"

No answer. She should have responded by now.

Where are you?

The landscaping that once offered serene privacy now provided countless hiding spots. I scanned the area, noting every potential refuge: an overturned cabana, the shadows beneath a row of hibiscus bushes, the space behind a decorative fountain where someone small could tuck themselves away.

"Olivia!" My voice broke, betraying the terror that was creeping into the edges of my focus.

Get it together, Eva Rae. She's counting on you.

"Mom!" I spun on my heel, the sound slicing through the gunfire and hysteria.

"Here!" Fainter this time, but unmistakably Olivia. I locked onto the direction, sprinting past a grove of palm trees.

"Stay put, baby, I'm coming!"

My legs burned, and my heart pounded a relentless rhythm—one I couldn't afford to silence until I had her safe.

I rounded a corner, nearly colliding with a woman in a blood-stained sundress. Her eyes were wild, her breathing erratic.

"Where did he go?" I demanded, gripping her shoulders to steady us both.

"Th-that way," she stammered, pointing shakily. "He was shooting… at everyone."

"Stay down and find cover," I instructed, releasing her with a firm nod.

"Be careful," she whispered as if the words were torn from her lips.

The resort was unrecognizable; scenes of leisure turned into vignettes of violence. The air was thick, and the tang of gunpowder overpowered the salt breeze. Overturned lounge chairs formed an obstacle course that I navigated with grim determination while panic raged in my heart.

"Olivia!"

My throat was raw, but I couldn't stop calling for her. Each overturned chair and every shattered vase had me expecting the worst, yet I prayed for the best.

A cluster of guests cowered behind a toppled tiki bar, their whispers urgent and low. I skirted around them without slowing, my senses on high alert. There was no time for reassurance or comfort; there was only the mission—find Olivia, stop Marcus.

I rounded a corner, pulse hammering in my ears, and nearly

tripped over a young man sprawled across the path. Blood seeped through his fingers as he clutched at his arm, face contorted.

"Stay with me," I said, dropping to a knee beside him.

"Help," he gasped, eyes wild with shock.

"Press here, hard," I instructed, guiding his other hand to apply pressure. "It's just a graze. You're going to make it."

I scanned the area once more for Olivia, then pushed to my feet, leaving him with a nod of encouragement. I had to move; every second was critical.

Dodging through a maze of debris, I caught a glimpse of Marcus ahead. His back was to me, fingers working frantically to reload. Time slowed as I ducked behind a stone pillar, barely breathing. Options flickered through my mind—rush him, distract him, negotiate? No, too risky with the weapon in play.

"Think, Eva," I muttered, watching his shoulders tense with each click of the ammunition. My window of opportunity was closing fast.

The pillar chilled my back through the fabric of my blazer as I crouched, heart a metronome in double time. Marcus's shadow stretched toward me, sinister and elongated on the sun-soaked ground.

A rustle to my left snapped me back to the present. A cluster of guests, their faces etched with terror, huddled like scared hatchlings beneath an overhanging palm. I darted toward them.

"Have you seen my daughter?" I barked, my voice as hard as flint. "Short hair, about this tall. Seen her?"

Their eyes flicked between each other, lips quivering, whispers frantic as a disturbed beehive. Finally, one—a woman with mascara streaks down her cheeks—nodded, jerking her head in the direction of the beach.

"She ran that way," she stammered, voice barely above the din.

"Stay down," I ordered, more bark than bite, already moving. "Keep quiet."

I wove through the chaos, the tableau of destruction imprinted behind my eyelids—every cry, every plea, a siren call to action.

The scent of gunpowder lingered in the air as I approached the beach, a mocking contrast to the tropical paradise that had turned into a hunting ground.

My legs pumped harder, each stride a silent vow.

Olivia, just hold on.

The path to the beach was a blur of green and brown, fronds whipping at my arms as I dodged through the landscaped maze. Every shout behind me and every scream tightened the air in my chest.

"Marcus!" I called out, half-hoping he'd reveal himself, half-dreading the same. No answer, but the roar of the ocean grew louder and more insistent with each step I took.

"Olivia!" I shouted her name into the wind, willing it to carry, to find her, to wrap her in safety. My heart thrashed against my ribs, a caged bird desperate for release.

The beach unfolded before me, a stretch of pristine white sand marred by the day's horrors. I scanned the horizon, every shadow, every rock, searching for her, for any sign.

Stay sharp, Eva. She's here. She has to be.

"Please," I whispered to no one, to everyone.

Let her be safe.

Sand flew beneath my feet as I emerged onto the beach, eyes darting from one potential hiding place to another. The ocean's rhythm played a deceptive lullaby against the distant staccato of gunfire.

Where are you, Olivia?

"Olivia!" My voice cut through the chaos, a blade seeking its mark.

There! A figure huddled behind a massive rock, shoulders heaving with shallow breaths. Her form was unmistakable, even from a distance—Olivia. Relief washed over me in an over-whelming wave; it took everything not to collapse under its weight. But something was wrong.

"Mom!" Her cry was a thin thread of sound.

I tore across the sand, heart hammering as fear clawed its way back up my throat. Close now, I could see the crimson stain spreading across her arm.

She'd been shot.

Chapter 36

I SETTLED beside Olivia on the jagged surface of the rock. Olivia's silhouette was hunched, a figure carved from shadows and pain against the backdrop of Paradise Key's faux tranquility. My gaze traced the line of crimson that ran down her arm.

"Hey," I murmured, reaching for her wounded arm with hands that had steadied guns and soothed skinned knees with equal proficiency. "It's just a graze. You're going to be alright."

She didn't lift her head, but her hands dropped, revealing eyes red-rimmed and haunted. The bullet might have only kissed her skin, but something deeper had been punctured.

"Olivia." My voice was soft yet carried the weight of a mother's heart. I rested my hand between her shoulder blades, feeling the tremors coursing through her.

"Mom," she whispered.

"It's okay," I said, giving her space to breathe, to piece herself back together.

She exhaled a shaky breath that carried the weight of untold stories. "That night," Olivia started, "with Mark... the beach was ours."

I watched her closely. Her hands, once steady, now trembled as if they held the fragile pieces of her heart.

"Go on," I urged, my tone a tempered blend of command and comfort.

"Mark... You were right; we were together." The words spilled out haltingly. "The sand was cool, the stars like a blanket over us." She paused, gulping air as if it could fill the void Mark left behind.

"Olivia." My prompt was soft, yet insistent.

"His skin," she continued, "was warm against mine, alive with every heartbeat." I sensed the raw passion that had fueled their forbidden rendezvous, the urgency that pulsed beneath Olivia's confession.

"Then what happened?" I steered her gently back to the path of her recollection.

"He rejected me." The words hung in the air, stark and unembellished. "We were kissing and holding hands. But then, suddenly, he just... turned cold. Said things. Mean things. Hurtful things. He didn't want to be like me. He wasn't like me, he said. I didn't understand. Up until then, he had seemed to be into me. Flirting, and then the kissing. How could that be nothing?" Pain etched deeper lines into Olivia's youthful face, a sorrow that seemed to transcend the physical pain.

I pieced it together—the heated whispers, the touch of skin on skin, and then the icy aftermath. Probably fueled by a mother who had other plans for him.

"Doesn't sound like it was nothing," I said. "Sounds like he was scared, perhaps."

"Scared of what?" she said, then broke down in tears. "I didn't... I don't understand what I did wrong."

"Hey." I drew her in close, my arm a shield around her quaking shoulders. "It's okay. Let it out."

"Mark told me...." Olivia's voice was a serrated edge, sawing through the silence. "...I was nothing. A mistake."

That word, "mistake," struck a chord, reverberating through my entire being. I tightened my hold, anger and sorrow warring within me. Mark's rejection was a wound far deeper than any graze from a bullet.

"Olivia. He was wrong." My words came out measured, each one deliberate.

"Was he?" Doubt clouded her eyes.

"Absolutely."

I hated that she hadn't felt she could tell me this earlier. Had I not been listening? Should I have seen this? Guilt gnawed at my insides as I watched her struggle, her pain a tangible thing between us. I wished I could take it away, all the pain.

"Mom...."

"Shh, I'm here," I murmured, but the comfort sounded hollow to my own ears. I had been there yet so far away.

"Sorry," she mumbled, looking away. "I don't know who I am anymore. I'm so sorry."

"No, Liv, I—" A knot of sadness lodged in my throat. "You have nothing to be sorry for."

She drew in a shuddering breath, lifting her head from her hands.

"Mom, what if they all judge me?"

The fear in her voice cut through the silence like a knife. "I thought if I stopped Marcus, then maybe they'd stop thinking bad of me. That's why I ran after him, but he shot me, and now I'm... I did nothing. I changed nothing."

"Let them try." My words, firm and sharp, sliced the night air. "You have me, Liv. No matter what."

"Even if—" Her sentence hung unfinished, choked by the unspoken. "They think I killed him? That's why I didn't tell you or anyone else what happened that night. I thought they'd think I killed him because of his rejection."

"Let them try," I repeated, my support unwavering.

"But the blood...." A single tear traced its way down her cheek. "You saw the blood. On my shirt."

"Tell me where it came from."

"We went to the small pier. We sat down, and there was a nail sticking out—an old rusty one. He cut his finger on it when leaning back on his hand. It was bleeding, so I took off my T-shirt and gave it to him. I was, after all, wearing a bikini underneath, so it wasn't a big deal. I let him wrap it around his finger until the blood stopped. He threw it back at me when we got into the fight, and I took it and ran. I swear that's what happened. I didn't think anyone would believe me."

I reached for her hand, grasping it tightly. "I believe you. Someone else killed him. Mark's gone, but you're here. Alive. And that's what counts."

"Is it enough?" Doubt laced her words, a whisper barely audible above the rustle of palm trees.

"More than enough." I held her gaze, willing her to believe. "You're enough."

Olivia nodded slowly, her eyes holding mine. "I just don't understand why anyone would want to hurt him—"

"Me neither." I cut her off, not wanting her to spiral again. "But we'll figure it out. I promise you."

"Okay." It was a frail agreement, but it was something.

Silence settled between us, but my mind raced, piecing together Olivia's jagged confession with the island's grim past.

Chapter 37

The low murmur of conversation faded as Isla ascended the narrow wooden staircase leading to the attic. She brushed past cobwebs draped like gossamer veils from the rough-hewn beams, her heart aching for solace. The oppressive weight of another awful dinner's tension seemed to lift slightly with each step away from the dining room battlefield. She decided to go where she used to hide from her mother's wrath as a child.

As she emerged into the attic, Isla inhaled deeply, the smell of aged wood and long-forgotten memories filling her senses. Moonlight spilled through a small window, casting ethereal patterns upon the floor. Dust motes danced in the air, disturbed by her presence in this seldom-visited space. Isla moved with purpose, navigating between boxes filled with relics of her family's past, seeking a haven where thoughts could roam free without the scrutiny of Victoria's gaze. The old photo albums. They had always been able to cheer her up.

In the far corner, beneath a draped sheet, Isla's fingers found the edge of an old chest she hadn't noticed before. She pulled it aside and opened it, revealing a leather-bound album wedged between stacks of yellowing newspapers and discarded trinkets.

The cover creaked open, protesting years of neglect. Isla's eyes widened as they fell upon the first photograph—an image of a much younger Victoria, her hair styled in soft waves framing her striking features. But it wasn't her mother's youthful beauty that captured Isla's attention; it was the man standing beside Victoria, his arm looped casually around her waist, their smiles easy and genuine.

Who was this man whose laughter seemed to leap from the page? Isla's breath hitched as she turned the pages, each photo a window into a life her mother had never spoken of. There were candid shots of the pair lounging on sun-drenched beaches, sipping coffee at quaint sidewalk cafes, and dancing under strings of twinkling lights. In every image, Victoria's ice-blue eyes held warmth, a stark contrast to the coldness Isla knew all too well.

A whisper of paper signaled a hidden compartment at the back of the album. Isla eased out an envelope, its seal already broken. Inside, a smaller photo revealed the two of them together, their foreheads touching, lost in a moment of shared secrets. The intimacy of the gesture prompted a flurry of questions to rise within Isla, her mind racing to piece together the fragments of her mother's concealed history.

Clutching the album to her chest, Isla leaned back against the cool wall, the moon now a silent confidant to her discovery. What stories lie behind these frozen moments? What had led Victoria to tuck them away in the shadows of the attic, buried beneath layers of dust and time?

The photographs—each a silent testament to an unspoken past—whispered tales that Isla's heart yearned to decipher. A younger Victoria, her mother's features softened by time, smiled back at her, not with the strained expression Isla had come to expect but with genuine joy. Who was this man who stood beside her mother, their camaraderie captured as though it were the most natural thing in the world?

Questions swirled in Isla's mind. It seemed impossible that the stony, unyielding matriarch downstairs was once this carefree soul, her arms wrapped around a stranger who exuded an air of significance.

Determination rose within Isla. The album before her was a puzzle, and she was certain its pieces were crucial to understanding the problems between her and Victoria. Her mother's guarded eyes and tight-lipped stories had left a void filled only with conjecture, but now there was a glimmer of something tangible—a lead to follow, a history to unearth.

"Who are you?" Isla whispered into the darkness, speaking to the shadows of her mother's former self.

Isla rose, her silhouette a faint outline against the attic window, the photo album cradled like a precious relic against her chest. Whatever secrets lay nestled within Victoria's history, Isla was determined to bring them into the light.

Chapter 38

I FELT it before I saw anything—the charged silence, the way the air seemed to constrict around us. The shooting had stopped. But where was he? Where was Marcus Cole? I felt an unease spread inside of me. Every nerve ending was alight with the knowledge that Marcus could be watching, his presence a shadow lurking nearby.

"Mom?" Olivia's voice was barely audible over the rustle of the palms.

"Stay close." My words cut through the balmy breeze, my hand reaching back to find hers. "We need to get out of here."

We moved with purpose, our footsteps soft against the stone pathway. Each flicker of light from the torches cast elongated shadows that danced ominously around us. I couldn't shake the feeling of eyes tracking our every step, the cold certainty that we were not alone in this tropical paradise turned sinister.

"Olivia." I kept my voice level. "We need to think like he does—stay one step ahead."

She nodded, her silhouette tense beside me. The glint of determination in her eyes reminded me so much of myself at that age—fearless, even when fear was the most sensible thing to feel.

"Let's—" Her breath hitched as she stumbled against an uneven edge of the path.

"Careful," I whispered, steadying her with a firm grip.

"Sorry," she murmured, straightening up.

"Nothing to apologize for." The words were automatic, but they carried weight.

Her body leaned into mine, seeking solace. I wrapped my arm around her, feeling the tremble in her frame. She was strong, my girl, but even the strongest need a haven.

"Mom," she said, her voice muffled against my shoulder. "I don't know if I can—"

"You can," I interrupted, fierce and certain. "You're stronger than you realize."

"Thanks," she breathed, pulling back slightly to look at me. There was a spark there, a kindling of resolve.

"Let's keep moving," I urged, my voice low. Time was slipping through our fingers, each second a drumbeat toward an unknown climax.

"Right behind you," she affirmed, and I felt the subtle shift in her stance—a readiness that matched my own.

I glanced at the sky, noting how the dark clouds mirrored the churn in my gut. Marcus was still out there—cunning, damaged, and unpredictable. My mind raced with scenarios, each more harrowing than the last.

"Mom," Olivia's voice cut through my spiraling thoughts. "What's our next move?"

"Find him before he finds us," I replied tersely, my eyes never leaving the horizon and the darkening sky. "We don't have much time."

She nodded, her lips pressed into a thin line. Her hands were fists at her sides, ready for whatever came next. I admired her courage, her resilience—a chip off the old block.

"Olivia," I said sharply, grabbing her attention. "Remember, no hesitations. We do what we must to stay safe."

"I understand," she responded, her tone laced with steel.

"Good." I scanned our surroundings, every sense heightened.

The Paradise Key had turned into a chessboard, and we were pawns in Marcus's twisted game.

"Mom…" Olivia began, her eyes searching mine.

"Say it," I prompted, knowing unspoken fears festered worse than open wounds.

"Are you scared?" Her voice barely rose above the wind picking up around us.

"Terrified," I admitted. It wasn't weakness to acknowledge fear; it was foolishness to ignore it. "But fear keeps us sharp. And I'll be damned if I let that man harm you more than he has already."

Olivia stepped closer, her shoulder brushing against mine. The silent message was clear—we were in this together, come hell or high water.

"Let's end this," she whispered, her determination tangible.

I nodded slowly, feeling the weight of our plight. The clouds grew heavier as if they, too, anticipated the coming confrontation. We shared a look that needed no translation—it was time to act.

Chapter 39

THEN:

The screen door of Aunt Bea's quaint cottage slapped shut with an urgency that immediately made her look up from the book she was reading just as Isla burst through. Her chest heaved with the exertion of her sprint, eyes ablaze with the kind of fierce excitement that comes from unearthing secrets long buried. The photo album in her grasp bore the brunt of her tight grip.

"Aunt Bea, you have to see what I found!" she exclaimed, words stumbling into the warm space like eager children.

"Slow down, dear," Aunt Bea said, her voice the embodiment of the serene haven she provided within these walls. She peered over the rim of her glasses with eyes that had seen much and missed little.

Isla drew a quick breath, struggling to rein in her whirlwind thoughts enough to articulate them. "It's—it's about Mom."

She unfolded the album, her fingers trembling. "There are things here, things she never told us. Secrets."

The young woman's revelations spilled forth, each word piling onto the last with a fervency that left little room for pause.

Aunt Bea absorbed the torrent of information, her face a canvas of calm where worry lines softened rather than furrowed. She exhaled softly, the sound carrying with it a weight of decades.

"Your mother," she began, her voice steady but tinged with an undercurrent of sorrow. "She didn't always have the... rigidity she wears like armor now." Aunt Bea paused, her gaze drifting toward the window.

Isla's hands stilled their restless movement, her body leaning forward instinctively as Aunt Bea's words promised a glimpse into the enigma that was Victoria.

"There was a time," Aunt Bea continued, the lenses of her glasses capturing the light from her reading lamp, "when a young Victoria brimmed with dreams, much like you. But life, Isla, has a way of testing us, molding us with fire and ice."

She spoke of a summer long ago, of a young girl with laughter in her eyes and love on her lips. A summer that turned to ash when a careless whisper became a roar of disapproval, tearing apart the tender fabric of a first love deemed unsuitable by family decree.

"Victoria had a choice to make," Aunt Bea said, the lines around her eyes deepening with the memory. "Conformity or defiance. In the end, she chose the path laid out for her, not the one she yearned to tread."

Listening, Isla felt the room around her grow still, the tick of the clock receding into silence. The image of her mother, so often cast in the role of the oppressor, began to shift and morph. Behind the ice-blue eyes and cool reproach lay a history of hurt, a legacy of love lost and walls built to endure.

"Her heart was broken," Isla murmured, the insight dawning like a slow sunrise over her features. Her own heart, so full of youthful passion and desire, ached at the thought of her mother enduring such pain.

"Yes," Aunt Bea confirmed, her tone imbued with the understanding that comes from witnessing the fractures in another's soul. "And sometimes, broken hearts heal crooked, leaving the shards to cut anew with every beat."

A resolve blossomed within Isla then, a resilient bud pushing through the cracks of a weathered stone. The revelation of her mother's trauma did not excuse the barriers Victoria erected between her and Javier, but it brought a depth of compassion Isla hadn't known she could feel for her mother.

"Then I will be different," Isla declared, her voice a low thrum of determination. "I'll fight for Javier, for us. No matter what shadows lurk in our family's past, I won't let them shape my future."

Aunt Bea nodded, pride and concern mingling in her wise eyes. "Just remember, love is both sword and shield. Wield it well, Isla."

With her aunt's blessing warming her spirit, Isla straightened her back. She was the same girl who had rushed into the room hours before, yet irrevocably changed—tempered in understanding and honed in purpose.

Chapter 40

I STOOD ON THE PRECIPICE, the edge of the main house. It was now dark outside, and the wind had picked up again. I had helped guests inside before the rain started and attended to people's wounds. I counted nine people in total that had been shot, and luckily, no one fatally. Fortunately, Marcus Cole was not a very good shot, or maybe he didn't really want to kill anyone, just hurt people in his act of rage. No matter what, he was still very dangerous and still out there somewhere. I called for help, and paramedics and police were on their way. Meanwhile, I needed to find out where Marcus was. We were like sitting ducks right now. I told Olivia to remain with the wounded and the rest of the guests, then ventured outside.

I arrived at the rocks down the beach, breath hitching, and my heart thudding against my ribs as if it were trying to escape.

"Marcus!" My voice cut through the howling wind.

I spotted him then, a lone figure etched against the dark sky, inches from oblivion. With his back to me, he stood defiantly at the edge of the precipice, shoulders hunched—a man burdened and on the brink. He was holding the gun, the barrel pressed against his temple.

"Marcus, don't do this," I called, firm but laced with concern. I couldn't let him become another casualty.

"Go away."

His words whipped back at me, almost lost in the wind.

"Talk to me. That's all I'm asking." My feet moved over the slick ground, cautious yet determined. Each of my senses was sharpened by the perilous dance of negotiation.

"There's nothing left to say," his voice strained, a razor's edge of despair cutting through.

He pivoted on his heels, the turmoil in his gaze a whirlpool of raw emotion. Anger and pain clashed.

"Marcus," I murmured, inching closer, feet finding purchase on the uncertain ground. "You've heard a thousand lies, felt a thousand letdowns. But you've got to know I'm not one of them."

"Easy for you to say." His voice, jagged with bitterness, cut through the wind's howl.

"Look at me," I insisted. "I see you, Marcus. Not the case number, not the headlines—just you. The kid who wanted more than the hand he was dealt."

"That kid's long gone," he spat, but his eyes wavered—searching mine. The gun in his hand was shaking.

"Then talk to me about the man standing here now," I pressed on, maintaining eye contact like it was our lifeline. "The one who survived when everything tried to break him."

"Survived?" He scoffed—a hollow sound. "You call this surviving? I just shot a bunch of people."

"Don't give up," I said, feeling the precarious balance between us.

"It ends here. It's for the best. Maybe it's what I deserve...."

"Stop." I reached out, not touching, just offering. "Don't you dare believe that. You deserve the truth. A chance."

"Chance...." His word lingered, a plea disguised as defiance.

"Right here, right now, Marcus. Take it."

The first heavy drops hit, fat and cold. The sky above Paradise Key Private Resort opened above us as yet another thunderstorm rolled in. The wind clawed at my jacket, flapping the fabric like a loose sail. I planted my feet on the slick stone, each step a gamble.

"Marcus!" My voice barely crested the growing roar of wind. "Think about what you're doing!"

"Thinking is all I've done," he yelled back, water streaming down his face, indistinguishable from tears.

"Violence won't bring Isla back," I said, advancing with care, feeling the rain turn the ground to soap beneath me. "It won't clear your name."

"Clear my name?" His laugh was a sharp crack, almost lost in the thunder. "And what? Go back to nothing?"

"Nothing can become something." I kept moving. "But only if you're alive to see it through."

"Alive…." He turned slightly, eyes wild, searching mine.

"Listen to me, Marcus." Rain plastered my hair to my scalp, and streams of water coursed down my back. "Isla wouldn't want this for you."

"You didn't know her!" he shot back, but his voice cracked, a fissure in his resolve.

"Then tell me," I urged. "Tell me who she was, what she stood for. Honor her memory the right way."

He paused. Tension knotted his brow, loosening and tightening as waves of indecision crashed over his features.

"Is this it?" I shouted over the wind's roar. "The end you pictured?"

His lips moved silently, wrestling with unseen ghosts. For a heart-beat, the hopeful boy peeked through the veil of the hardened man before me. He reached into his pocket, pulled out a note, and handed it to me.

"Read this when I'm gone."

"Marcus." My plea was raw.

Then, his face became set like stone. "No more words!" he spat, body coiling like a spring.

"Wait!"

I yelled.

But it was too late.

With a reckless energy, he pulled the trigger. Panic surged through me—a jolt of electricity.

"Marcus, no!"

I leaped, fingers snatching at the air, grasping. I grabbed him just as his lifeless body fell to the ground.

Chapter 41

THEN:

Victoria sat at her vanity, the soft glow of the morning sun spilling through the window and bathing her in an almost celestial light. Her hands rested gently on the mahogany surface, fingers tracing the intricate carvings as if to draw strength from their time-worn patterns. The mirror before her reflected an image of poise: a woman untroubled, with ice-blue eyes that held the world at bay and blonde hair swept up in a bun so perfect it defied any suggestion of haste.

But behind those eyes raged something sinister, thoughts swirling around the decision she had reached—a decision she believed was an act of mercy, a necessity. Victoria's heart thrummed with the rhythm of inevitability as she considered Isla, her own flesh and blood. The girl threatened the very fabric of their existence with her recklessness, her untamed spirit. Victoria felt compelled to act to save the family from scandal and the shame of Isla's forbidden love for Javier. In her mind, it was the only way to salvage their legacy.

"Mother?" The voice was soft, barely above a whisper, but it cut through Victoria's reverie like a knife through silk.

Isla stood at the threshold, her brown hair cascading over slender shoulders, her figure poised tentatively as if unsure of her welcome. Sunlight caught in her hair, setting it ablaze with hues of copper and gold.

"Darling," Victoria replied, her voice smooth as velvet, betraying none of the turmoil that churned within. "Do come in."

Isla's gaze lingered on her mother, searching, hoping. She stepped inside, the hem of her dress whispering against the floor as she moved closer. She carried an old photo album in her hands, one that Victoria knew all too well. Seeing this again made her heart stop for a second before she composed herself.

"I wanted to talk to you, Mother," Isla said, placing the album in front of her. "About... everything."

"Of course," Victoria said, turning in her chair to face her daughter fully, masking the calculating glint in her eye with a serene smile. "I've been reflecting on recent events myself."

"Really?" Isla's voice lifted, tinged with a fragile optimism. "I hope we can find our way back to how things were. I miss us, Mother—I miss our talks, the way you would guide me."

"Life is an ever-changing tapestry, my dear. We must all adapt to the new patterns it presents us."

Victoria's words flowed like sweet nectar, laced with an undercurrent of something darker that Isla, in her yearning for reconciliation, did not detect.

"Then, do you think... Do you think you could accept Javier? Accept us?" Isla asked, her hands clasped together as if in silent prayer.

"Let us focus on one step at a time, Isla," Victoria counseled, her calm exterior a stark contrast to the decisive coldness that had settled in her heart. "How about you and I go for a walk on the beach? We can have a picnic."

"I would love that. Thank you, Mother," Isla breathed out, her relief palpable. Her eyes were alight with a hope that danced dangerously close to the precipice of her mother's concealed intentions.

Leaning against the cool marble of the hallway, Marcus Cole's gaze lingered on the partially open door to Victoria's bedroom. From this discreet vantage point, he could see Isla, her back turned toward him as she conversed with Victoria. But it wasn't the sight of them together that troubled him; it was the things being said. It was too smooth, too rehearsed. It hung in the air like a velvet curtain, concealing the truth behind its plush facade.

"Something isn't right," Marcus muttered under his breath, the knot in his stomach tightening with every honeyed word that dripped from Victoria's lips. He knew the cadence of deception all too well, and it echoed through Victoria's calculated responses. There was an art to her duplicity that played out before Isla in a performance worthy of the grandest stages.

"Focus on one step at a time, Isla," Victoria's voice floated through the gap, each syllable measured, each pause deliberate.

Marcus furrowed his brow, his concern for Isla amplifying into a silent alarm. He had seen Victoria's charm wielded like a weapon, but never with such dangerous precision.

"I need to keep an eye on them both," he resolved, the weight of his responsibility pressing upon him with newfound urgency. He loved Isla with everything he had and vowed to protect her.

The soft crush of wet sand beneath her feet brought a rare moment of solace to Isla as she ventured out on her walk with her mother. The ocean's rhythmic hush seemed to whisper encouragement, the gentle touch of the breeze playing with her long hair. She replayed the morning's conversation with Victoria in her mind, dissecting each word, each pause, searching for signs of thaw in her mother's frosty demeanor.

Maybe she's finally seeing things differently, Isla thought to herself, allowing a fragile tendril of hope to unfurl within her chest.

It was a hope tinged with naivety—the kind that painted the world in forgiving strokes—a hope that Victoria might come to understand Isla's love for Javier, that love that transcended the rigid lines drawn by her family's expectations.

In the distance, unnoticed by Isla and her mother, Marcus trailed behind, his polished shoes sinking slightly into the damp sand. He watched Isla with a furrowed brow, the weight of his concerns growing heavier with each step she took. There were moments when he wanted to call out to warn her, but he held back, trapped in hesitation.

Marcus had seen it—the subtle shift in Victoria's gaze when she looked at Isla as if measuring the worth of her daughter through a lens smeared with disdain.

And he feared the worst was about to happen.

Chapter 42

THE DOOR swung open with a creak that echoed through the main house like a gunshot. I stepped inside, rainwater streaming off my jacket, forming puddles on the polished marble floor. Their eyes, those of the wounded and the weary, clung to me like ivy. Hope wrestled with fear in their gazes, an unspoken plea hanging in the charged air.

"Marcus is dead," I said, cutting through the thick silence without warning.

A collective breath left the room as if the walls themselves exhaled. Heads bowed, shoulders dropped—an invisible weight seemed to lift, if only for a heartbeat.

"Dead?" The word rebounded off the high ceilings, a whisper amplified into a scream by someone's disbelief. It was my friend Amy.

"By his own hand," I confirmed. My voice didn't waver, though my legs threatened to buckle beneath me.

"Are you certain?" The question came from the back, timid yet demanding confirmation.

"Positive." There was no energy left in me for softness. "I saw him. He left us… a note."

"Jesus..." Someone else muttered—a prayer or a curse, I couldn't tell which.

"Is this over then?" Doubt laced the tentative inquiry.

"Far from it." I scanned their faces, each one a story marred by the night's grim revelations. "We've still got a killer among us."

A blur of motion broke from the crowd, and Olivia was at my side in an instant. Her arms wrapped around me with a fierceness that defied her slender frame, and for a brief moment, I let myself lean into her embrace. The warmth of her body seeped through my wet clothes.

"Mom," she said, her voice taut with barely contained emotion. My heart clenched at the sound, so full of worry and care.

She stepped back just enough to look at me, her eyes scanning my face as if trying to read the story etched in the lines of my weariness.

"Are you okay?"

I met her gaze and saw the flicker of pain that she couldn't hide, the bloody wound on her shoulder a stark reminder of the brutality she had faced. I wanted to offer her comfort, to be the pillar of strength she sought, but the truth weighed heavy on my tongue.

"No, Liv, I'm not," I admitted, my voice low, betraying the fatigue that pulled at my bones. Her eyes, so much like mine, filled with understanding—and something else, a resolve that matched my own.

"Talk to me, Mom," Olivia said, her gaze insistent, slicing through the layers of my resolve. "What happened out there?"

I exhaled, shoulders slumping as if the weight of the events could be shaken off. My hand dipped into my jacket pocket, fingers brushing against crumpled paper. Withdrawing the note, I felt its edges damp from the rain but no less significant.

"Marcus... he gave me this." My voice was a whisper, yet it carried, amplified by silence and gravity. "I read it as soon as he... died."

Her eyes flickered with trepidation as I unfolded the note, every pair of eyes in the room drawn to the once-hidden words now laid bare for all to witness. I scanned the message quickly, each word etching itself into my memory, a loud echo of Marcus's voice.

The script was sharp, hurried—written by a man aware that time was slipping through his fingers. I read aloud, my voice steady despite the anger brewing within me,

"'So many lies. So many lives hurt. It ends here.'"

Murmurs swelled around us, a crescendo of dread and curiosity that filled the spaces between our breaths. The note trembled slightly in my grip.

"What is it, Mom? What does it say?" Olivia pressed, her voice a beacon of urgency in the whispers.

The note's words echoed in my mind, a haunting refrain. I lifted my gaze, letting it sweep over the anxious faces before me. They blurred into a single tapestry of guilt and suspicion until my eyes landed on one figure—still, watchful—a shadow among shadows.

"Tell me," I began, my voice slicing through the hush. "When did you decide their lives were expendable? Isla, Mark, and, in the end, Marcus?"

The individual met my stare, unflinching. The room's air crackled, charged with the collective inhale of shocked breaths, waiting, expecting.

"Isla, Mark, Marcus—all dead because of what?"

Silence answered me, heavy and opaque. I stepped closer. "Speak."

No movement. No remorse flickered across the face, only a cold calculation that sent shivers down my spine.

"Three people," I pressed, every word etched with resolve. "Three lives taken. And for what? Why?"

Stillness enveloped the space as if the very walls leaned in to hear the confession that refused to come. I waited, my pulse thrumming a relentless rhythm against my temples.

"Answer me!"

The demand tore from my lips, raw and insistent. The room held its breath, the truth an elusive specter dancing just out of reach.

The room was a minefield of rapid heartbeats and shallow breaths, everyone anticipating the next move in a game where the stakes had never been higher. The person stood motionless, a statue among the living, shrouded in mystery and malice.

"Speak," I demanded once more.

Chapter 43

THEN:

As they trod the narrow path to the secluded cove, Isla's sandals left shallow impressions in the soft sand. The woven picnic basket swung gently in her grip, its contents carefully selected with Clementine as peace offerings—a symbol of her hope that today might pave the way for healing. Each step brought with it the promise of new beginnings.

"Remember when I taught you to swim?" Victoria's voice, smooth like the sea glass that Isla used to collect, broke the rhythm of their footsteps. "You were such a brave little thing, eager to chase the waves."

Isla glanced at her mother, walking beside her, noting how the sunlight played on Victoria's coiffed blonde hair, giving her an almost ethereal halo. Despite the years and tension that lay between them, there was something in Victoria's tone today—a warmth Isla hadn't felt since those carefree days of her youth.

"Brave? I remember being terrified," Isla said, allowing herself a small laugh, "but you wouldn't let go until I was paddling on my own." She shifted the basket to her other arm, the corners of her lips lifting into a hopeful smile.

"Of course not," Victoria replied with a soft chuckle that seemed to dance on the breeze. "I knew you could do it. You've always had this... incredible determination, Isla. Even as a child."

The words, so full of apparent pride and affection, wrapped around Isla like a warm towel after a brisk swim. She yearned to sink into the comfort of those memories, to believe in the picture of maternal love that Victoria painted with her carefully chosen words.

"Those days were special," Isla murmured, her eyes lingering on the horizon—a vast canvas of blue that mirrored her deep longing for connection.

Isla's response came in the form of a smile, vulnerable and tender, as she listened to Victoria's recollections. Her eyes, bright with a hint of unshed emotion, reflected the turmoil of hope and hurt that danced within her—a craving for the maternal bond she had once cherished. With each step toward the cove, Isla allowed herself to drift on the currents of possibility, adrift in the notion that perhaps the rift between them was not so vast after all.

"Really, it wasn't all bad, was it?" Isla ventured softly, her voice threading through the air. "Those days... they meant everything to me."

They emerged into the cove, where the scene unfolded like a carefully crafted painting. The narrow path gave way to an expanse of sand, nestled between craggy cliffs that stood sentinel over the secluded spot. Gentle waves lapped at the shore in rhythmic whispers, their frothy edges kissed by the sun's golden glow. The water shimmered, a tapestry of light and motion, inviting and serene.

The tranquility of the setting belied the tension that hummed between Isla and Victoria like a taut string. It was there, in the subtlest stiffening of Victoria's posture, the almost imperceptible tightening around her eyes. Yet Isla, caught up in her own reverie, failed to perceive the undercurrents that flowed just beneath the surface of their conversation. She took in the cove with an artist's appreciation, allowing the beauty to fill her senses, her heart momentarily lifted in hope.

Victoria unfurled a blanket with a fluid motion, the fabric billowing briefly before settling upon the fine sand. With a grace that seemed at odds with her internal disquiet, she gestured for Isla to join her.

"Let's sit, darling," she said, her voice soft.

Isla sank onto the blanket. The sand beneath conformed to her shape, offering an embrace she hadn't felt in years—not since those careless, sun-soaked days of her childhood. She watched her mother's every move, the elegance with which Victoria crossed her legs and smoothed the skirt of her dress, an action as practiced and precise as a dance.

"Remember when you used to build castles right over there?" Victoria began, pointing toward a craggy part of the beach where the sand was damp and malleable. "You were quite the architect, even then."

Isla's lips curved into a hesitant smile as she recalled hours spent shaping towers and moats, determined to create a fortress.

"I thought I could stop the ocean," she confessed, her eyes reflecting the mirth of the memory.

"Perhaps in your heart, you believed you could," Victoria replied, her tone soothing. "You've always had a strong will. Mark, your younger brother, is nothing like you. He takes after your father. Those two are like peas in a pod. I guess that's why they prefer each other's company, and he stayed with him back in New York for the summer. But you, you're like me. Always have been."

As Victoria continued to recount anecdotes laced with nostalgia, Isla found herself transported to a time before the distance, before the silence that had wedged itself between them. Each word from her mother was a hand extended in what appeared to be reconciliation, and Isla, hungering for this connection, clung to them like lifelines.

"Those summers… they were magical, weren't they?" Victoria murmured, a master of narrative painting images of a past untainted by the complexities of their present reality.

"Very much so," Isla agreed, her guard dissolving like sugar in warm water. She leaned back on her hands, allowing herself to bask in the glow of her mother's attention, the stories wrapping around her, soft and inviting. There, on that blanket, with the whispers of the ocean as their soundtrack, it was all too easy for Isla to listen— and to hope.

The rhythmic cadence of the waves provided a natural lull, and for a brief moment, the world seemed to pause. Isla turned her gaze toward the horizon, where the sky kissed the ocean in a seamless blend of colors. The cove's secluded embrace offered a rare solitude that encouraged contemplation. There was a palpable stillness as Isla allowed herself to imagine a future where her love for Javier wasn't cloaked in shadows but celebrated in the sun's full splendor.

Her heart dared to swell with hope, each beat a drum heralding change. Could this gentle conversation with Victoria signal a new beginning? Might the fractures in their relationship finally mend, allowing Isla the freedom to share the depths of her affection for Javier openly? The mere thought sent a flutter through her chest, a bird yearning to soar.

"Tell me about your life now, Isla." The soft inquiry sliced through the silence as naturally as a sailboat cutting through calm waters. Victoria's voice retained its soothing timbre, yet there was something else there—an undercurrent of curiosity that went unnoticed by Isla.

"Life is... good," Isla replied hesitantly, not quite ready to disrupt the fragile peace with the weight of her secrets. "School's fine. And my art, it's going well." She kept her words vague, clinging to the remnants of serenity the silence had offered.

"That's wonderful to hear." Victoria's response was light and airy, yet her eyes were sharp and analytical—scanning Isla's face for something unspoken, an artist herself seeking truth within abstract strokes. "And your friends?" she pressed further, her fingers idly trailing patterns in the sand, each line a subtle probe.

Isla drew in a breath, considering how much to reveal, the warmth of the sun on her back urging her toward transparency.

"They're great, supportive..." Her voice trailed off.

"What are your dreams? For the future?" her mother asked.

Isla looked at her, wondering if this was an invitation to speak of Javier. Yet she didn't dare to. She didn't want to ruin the moment.

"Most of all," Isla said, a spark igniting in her words, "I dream of the ocean. It's like this constant presence in my life, a force that is both freeing and grounding." She scooped a handful of sand, letting it cascade between her fingers back to the earth. "The way the waves ebb and flow... it makes me feel like I can go anywhere, be anyone."

Victoria watched her daughter, her eyes following the dance of the granules as they fell. The sunlight played upon Isla's hair.

"Independence is important to you, isn't it?" Victoria asked, her voice softer than the breeze yet carrying an undertone that was hard and calculating.

"Absolutely," Isla replied, her gaze still fixed on the horizon. "It's everything. Being able to make my own choices and live life on my terms. I want to explore, to discover... not just follow a path laid out for me."

As Isla spoke of her desire for autonomy, a subtle shift occurred in Victoria. The ice-blue of her eyes darkened ever so slightly, their edges sharpening like the shards of a broken mirror. The maternal warmth that had once cradled her expressions receded, giving way to cold, meticulous scrutiny.

Isla continued, oblivious to the transformation before her. "I mean, don't you ever feel the pull of the unknown? The thrill of charting your own course?"

Victoria's lips curved into a half-smile that did not reach her eyes. "Of course, darling," she murmured, the word tasting of sweet poison. "But one must always be aware of the dangers that lurk beneath the surface."

Isla nodded, taking in her mother's words but too enthralled by her own vision of the future to truly hear the warning they carried. Her heart beat in time with the rhythm of the waves, each pulse a drumbeat heralding her dreams of freedom and adventure.

"Life's about taking chances, isn't it?" Isla's hands waved animatedly, sculpting her dreams into the salty air. "I just want to be true to myself, no matter what."

"Chances," Victoria echoed, her voice slicing through the fabric of the conversation with a sharper edge, "or recklessness?" The question, abrupt and barbed, hung heavily between them.

Isla's words stumbled to a halt, a frown creasing her sun-kissed forehead as she turned to face her mother. The shift in Victoria's tone was subtle but unmistakable, like an undercurrent that threatened to tug one's feet from beneath the surface of calm waters.

"Mother, I just mean that—" Isla started, her resolve wavering slightly under Victoria's dissecting gaze.

"Darling," Victoria interjected smoothly, though the silkiness of her voice did little to mask the steel beneath. "You must understand that every choice has its consequences. Do you truly believe your unconventional aspirations will lead to happiness?"

Isla swallowed, the taste of apprehension bitter on her tongue. She reached for safer topics, hoping to dilute the brewing storm with reminiscence. "Remember when you taught me to dance? How we laughed when I stepped on your toes?"

A practiced smile returned to Victoria's lips, yet it lacked the warmth of genuine amusement.

"Yes, those were simpler times." Her eyes, however, remained watchful, tracking Isla's every reaction like a hawk eyeing its prey.

"Is there nothing more you wish to say, Isla?" Victoria pressed, each word etched with a frost that contrasted sharply against the sun's caress on their skin.

"I... I... I know about you and that other man."

"What man?"

"The one in your photos in the attic," she said. "In the album."

That made her mother laugh. "Oh, him? He was a good friend. Until I met your dad, that is."

"Was that all he was? A friend?" Isla asked.

"Yes, a dear friend. But it could never be more."

"Why not? Why are you not still friends?"

"I don't want to talk about that."

"I want more," Isla said. "With... Javier."

Victoria's patience was getting frayed like the hem of a well-worn dress. The tender veneer of motherly affection she had donned for the outing began to peel away, unveiling the cold determination beneath her ice-blue eyes. Those eyes ensnared Isla's gaze, pinning her in place with an intensity that sent a shiver skittering down her spine.

Isla's breath hitched in her chest, the air around them growing heavy with unspoken truths. Her dreams of reconciliation were quickly dissipating like mist over the ocean. Victoria's shifting demeanor threatened to engulf her, yet she could not look away. Suddenly, Victoria rose to her feet, the fluidity of her movement betraying nothing of the anger brewing within. She extended a hand toward Isla—a gesture that once would have signified comfort, now fraught with enigmatic purpose.

"Come," she said, her voice a whisper lost to the breeze. "Walk with me to the water's edge."

The command hung between them, an invitation wrapped in a riddle, laced with an urgency that Isla felt in her very marrow. Standing tentatively, Isla brushed the sand from her sundress, her mind a maelstrom of confusion and apprehension. With each step toward the lapping waves, the sense of foreboding deepened. Victoria's back remained turned to her daughter, her posture rigid and unreadable as they approached the threshold where land surrendered to the ocean.

As they reached the water's edge, Victoria placed a hand on Isla's neck, a touch that sent shivers down her spine. Uneasy, Isla asked, "What are you doing, Mom?"

Victoria turned slightly, her eyes shadowed with a mix of determination and sorrow. "You shouldn't bother coming home," she said, her voice firm yet tinged with sadness. "You've brought us enough shame and disappointment. Don't ever come back."

Tears welled in Isla's eyes as she cried out, "I don't want to turn my back on my family. I don't want to lose you. Mom?"

Victoria's gaze softened for a moment, but her resolve was unyielding. "It's too late."

With that, Victoria turned and walked away, leaving Isla

standing alone, the waves whispering secrets at her feet. Isla's mind whirled with indecision, her heart torn between duty and desire. She stood there, lost in thought, when suddenly, a pair of hands grabbed her from behind, squeezing tightly around her throat, and she struggled, gasping for breath. The last thing she said before she died was one word, a name:

"Javier."

Chapter 44

"AND THEN SHE STOPPED BREATHING. I was too late to save her, even though I ran to her rescue from my hiding place, where I had been watching her and her mother. I screamed her name and ran to her, but there was nothing I could do. I yelled and screamed, but her killer stood cold as stone and simply stared at her dead body in the water, where she had been held down. Then she asked me to help her push the body out to sea. I couldn't believe what she was saying, what she was asking me to do."

I looked up from Marcus's letter at the woman standing before me. I continued reading.

"And then she told me to say it was me. At first, I refused, but Aunt Beatrice can be very persuasive, and she promised me that since I was a minor, I wouldn't get a long punishment, and once I got out, my mother would still be alive since the family would pay for all her surgeries and treatment. There was nothing I could do; there was no way to bring Isla back anyway. And finally, I accepted. I was crushed and broken, but at least this way, my mom would live. Aunt Beatrice was also the one who paid for me to come back to the island this weekend. She wanted me to point at Victoria and say she was the one who paid me back then. Aunt Beatrice killed Mark, too, and wanted it to look like it was her sister's doing. I can't live with myself any longer, having taken part in this. That's why I must say goodbye. There is nothing left for me here on this earth."

I folded the paper again with a deep sigh. "He signed it, Marcus Cole. That's all it says, but that's enough."

"It was you? You killed both of my children?" the scream came from Victoria, standing next to her sister. "Why? WHY?"

"I wanted them out of the way if you really want to know," Beatrice spat. "Just like I want you out of the picture. Our father is dying. If I got rid of your children and had you framed for murder, all the inheritance would be mine. It's that straightforward. I made sure to bring Javier or Emilio with me here, as I told him to call himself, so you wouldn't know who he really was. I knew he could testify to how you made sure he was thrown off the island back then, how you threatened Isla. Marcus would say you murdered Isla and paid him to take the fall. All suspicion would fall on you. I wouldn't even have to kill you. You'd be gone for the rest of your life."

Victoria gasped for air and placed a hand on her heaving chest. "You… you murdered my children for money?"

"As if you didn't want her out of the way," Beatrice said. "She brought shame on you and almost revealed your deep, dark secret. Why don't we talk about that then? Huh? How you found out that Javier was really the son of your secret lover? You knew that he was also the real father of Isla? You were pregnant when you got married, but never told anyone. Except for me. Luckily for you, Isla looked more like you with the blond hair and fair skin, but it never could hide the fact that Javier and Isla were, in fact, half-siblings, and that was why they could never be together. That's why you desperately tried to separate them. She brought shame on you, and you wanted her gone. If I hadn't killed her, you'd have to reveal your secret to her."

"I wanted her sent away. To leave the island, not die," Victoria said, tears streaming down her cheeks.

"Oh, don't give me that. You were relieved when she was gone."

"You're delusional. I can't believe this."

Beatrice's eyes glinted with a dangerous intensity as she reached for an old knife hanging on the wall, her fingers curling around the handle with deliberate slowness. She pressed the cold blade against Victoria's throat, her voice cutting through the stunned silence of the room.

"Nobody move, or she dies!" Beatrice hissed, her words sharp and deadly.

Frozen in horror, the crowd exchanged panicked glances, unable to tear their eyes away from the terrifying scene unfolding before them.

Just when it seemed all hope had faded, Olivia, with a determined look, darted forward from the shadows, her feet barely making a sound on the wooden floor.

"Not today, Beatrice!" she shouted, her voice resolute as she hurled herself at Beatrice, knocking her off balance. They both tumbled to the ground in a flurry of limbs, the knife clattering harmlessly across the floor.

I sprang into action, adrenaline surging as I joined Olivia, helping to pin Beatrice down.

"Stay still, Beatrice! It's over!" I commanded, my voice firm despite the chaos.

At that precise moment, the door burst open with a resounding crash, and paramedics and police officers flooded into the room, their presence a reassuring sight.

"Everyone stand back!" one of the officers ordered, his voice authoritative as they quickly moved to secure the scene. We let go of Beatrice, who rose to her feet.

As the chaos subsided, the room fell into an eerie silence, and Victoria's eyes locked onto the knife lying on the ground, its blade glinting menacingly under the dim light. She let out a shaky breath.

"I will have my revenge for my children. They will not die in vain," she whispered to herself, her voice quivering with raw emotion and steely resolve. Clutching the knife with a white-knuckled grip, she turned to face her sister. With fierce determination burning in her eyes, Victoria lunged forward, the blade slicing through the air as she attacked her sister, driven by a torrent of grief and betrayal.

Beatrice, caught off guard by Victoria's sudden attack, stumbled back, her eyes widening in terror. "Victoria, stop!" she cried, trying to defend herself against the relentless onslaught.

Olivia and I exchanged panicked glances, unsure of what to do. We knew Victoria was driven by grief, but if we didn't intervene, Beatrice could lose her life.

"No!" I shouted, lunging forward to grab Victoria's wrists, desperately trying to pry the knife away from her. She lunged again and slipped out of my grip. The knife cut into Beatrice's shoulder, and she let out a scream. I screamed, then grabbed her again and pulled her away.

"Stop it, Victoria! This won't solve anything!"

She fought against my grip with all her might, her eyes wild and unrecognizable. "I won't rest until I see justice for my children!" she screamed, her voice echoing through the room.

As the police officers swarmed in to subdue Victoria, Beatrice collapsed onto the floor, gasping for air.

I watched as Victoria was forcibly dragged away by the police officers, her cries for justice dying down to nothing more than a distant echo. The weight of the situation hit me like a ton of bricks, and I sank to my knees, burying my face in my hands to muffle my sobs. My heart ached for the family torn apart by deceit and betrayal. Olivia rushed to my side and hugged me tight.

As the paramedics attended to Beatrice's wounds and the police took her away and began their investigation, a silent understanding passed between my daughter and me.

We were forever changed by this dark story, but at least we still had one another, and for now, that was all we needed.

Epilogue

THE WHEELS of our sedan crunched over the familiar gravel as we pulled into the driveway of our Cocoa Beach home. The sun was dipping low, casting long shadows across the yard. Olivia's sigh mingled with the soft hiss of the engine as it died. We exchanged a look—tired eyes meeting, shared relief unspoken. We had stayed in the keys for two more days, helping the police. I had given them the letter that was left for me outside my bungalow, which I could only assume Beatrice had written to deter me from my investigation. My friends and I had parted amicably, but I wasn't sure I wanted to see them again after this. Emilio had finally gotten the closure he had been searching for so desperately, and as I hugged him goodbye, I could almost feel the relief coming from him. He was free at last and could let go of Isla, the great love of his life.

"Home," Olivia murmured, and I felt the word like a balm on my frayed nerves.

Matt stood in the doorway, the fading light framing him. His smile, warm and open, was all the welcome we needed.

"Hey," he called out, stepping down from the porch as we got out of the car. His approach was easy and unhurried, but his eyes held the intensity of concern.

"Hey," I echoed, my voice hoarse.

He reached us in two long strides, arms wide. His embrace engulfed us, strong and sure. Olivia leaned into his chest just a fraction of a second before I allowed myself to melt into his hold. Home wasn't just a place; it was this, right here.

"Everything's okay now," Matt whispered, his breath warm against my hair.

"Is it?" I managed a faint chuckle despite the tightness in my throat.

"Absolutely," he assured, his tone a soothing melody that made me believe it might just be true. "I saw you on TV explaining the case to the journalists during that press conference. You were amazing. You solved this case."

"Well, I had some help," I said, looking at Olivia."

"We've missed you," Olivia said, her voice muffled against his shirt.

"Missed you more," Matt replied.

I let out a breath I didn't realize I'd been holding, the weight on my shoulders beginning to lift, thread by thread. The chaos of Paradise Key and the scent of salt and secrets seemed to dissolve in the air around us, replaced by the safety of Matt's unwavering support.

"Let's go inside," I suggested, pulling back slightly to look at both of them. "I could kill for a cup of coffee."

"Or sleep," Olivia added, her smile weary but genuine.

"Both." Matt grinned. "I've got you covered."

And just like that, the world outside the embrace of our family faded into the background, irrelevant for the moment. We were together again, and that was all that mattered.

The front door swung open before our feet had the chance to grace the welcome mat. In a blur of limbs and laughter, Christine and Alex cascaded toward us like a wave building its energy far out at sea.

"Mom!" Christine's voice cut through the air. Her long frame navigated the chaos with an athlete's grace. She was a whirlwind of sun-streaked hair and tanned limbs.

"Christine," I said, my voice steadier than I felt.

"Look at you, the hero coming home!" Her eyes were alight with mischief and pride as she wrapped her arms around me. The contact was grounding, a reminder of the world outside the FBI badge.

"Hero?" I arched an eyebrow, easing out of her grip. "More like the weary traveler."

"Ha! Weary, maybe. But Mom, you cracked the case."

Her grin was infectious, her admiration clear even as she teased. "They'll be teaching this at Quantico soon, 'The Eva Rae Thomas Method.'"

"Let's not get ahead of ourselves," I deflected, though warmth bloomed in my chest at her words. I looked at Olivia. "It was team-work, as always."

"Teamwork led by Super Mom," she shot back. "Everyone is talking about you. Accept it; you're kind of a big deal."

"Kind of," I echoed, allowing a smile to play at the corners of my mouth. It felt good to laugh after everything that had transpired. Good to be home.

"Olivia, hey," Alex's voice was a soft undertone amid the clamor of our homecoming.

She turned, her face a canvas of bottled emotions.

"Are you okay?" he murmured, his brown eyes locking onto hers with an unwavering stillness that seemed to draw out her words. He'd always loved Olivia more than his other siblings, and seeing the concern in his eyes right now made my heart swell.

"Alex, it's just—" Olivia's lips trembled as she grappled for expression. "Everything was so close, too close."

He nodded, the weight of her fear acknowledged in the silence between them. His hand found her shoulder. He was becoming such a big boy now, almost a man.

"I'm glad you and Mom are both safe now," he said, his voice barely above a whisper but heavy.

A burst of giggles interrupted the solemn bubble they had created. Angel bounced into view, her curls a halo of disarray, and her cheeks streaked with the remnants of a marker masterpiece.

"Olivia!" she squealed, oblivious to the gravity of the moment. "Guess what? Mr. Darcy learned a new trick!"

"Mr. Darcy?" Olivia blinked away the last of her tears, a fragile smile taking form.

"Yep! He can dance now!" Angel beamed, twirling on the spot, her stuffed dolphin clutched in one hand like a partner in her impromptu ballet.

"Is that so?" I chimed in, the tension easing from my shoulders at the sight of Angel's innocence.

"Uh-huh! And he only stepped on my toes twice!" She held up two fingers, her wide grin infectious.

"Only twice?" Olivia laughed, the sound mingling with the warmth of our laughter. It was the balm we all didn't know we needed.

"Next time, I'll teach him to leap!" Angel declared, already lost in her next grand plan for Mr. Darcy.

"Leaping dolphins," Alex said, his quip drawing another round of chuckles. "Now, there's a show."

Angel pirouetted away, leaving behind the spark of lightness that always trailed in her wake. We watched her go, the room somehow brighter for her presence.

We crowded into the living room, a whirlwind of motion and murmurs. Alex flicked on the lamp in the corner, its warm glow spilling across the mismatched cushions. Christine tossed a knitted throw over Olivia's shoulders, tucking it with care.

"Feels good to be home," I said, sinking into the familiar embrace of the well-worn sofa. The scent of vanilla from a nearby candle mingled with the faint tang of salty ocean air that clung to us like a second skin.

"Better than good," Matt said, perching on the armrest beside me, his hand finding mine.

"Tea?" Christine offered, already halfway to the kitchen, her ponytail swishing with each step.

"Please," Olivia and Alex said in unison.

"Angel, help me find the cookies," Christine called out.

"Chocolate chip?" Angel's voice floated back, hopeful.

"Of course!"

I let my gaze drift over the scene: the soft yellow walls adorned with family photos, the shelves crammed with books and board games, the plants in every corner standing as silent, green sentinels. It was a stark contrast to the manicured austerity of Paradise Key, where every surface gleamed with impersonal perfection. But I would pick this any day over that lifestyle.

As conversation flowed, I leaned back, observing the faces I loved bathed in the warm glow of the overhead light. A sense of purpose swelled within me, reinforced by the laughter and shared glances. Each story told, each joke exchanged, threaded through me, stitching closed the wounds of uncertainty that had frayed my edges.

Here's to family," Matt said, raising his teacup. His voice was steady as a rock.

"To family," we echoed, the words a collective embrace.

After we had dinner and the children had scattered, I lingered at the table, tracing the wood grain with my finger. The weekend's trials seemed distant now, shadows chased away by the love of family. My heart beat with a renewed vigor, my resolve steeling for whatever lay ahead.

We would face it together, this family of mine. In the laughter, the tears, the mundane, and the profound—we were united. And nothing, not even the darkest of mysteries, could sever the ties that bound us.

THE END

Afterword

Dear Reader,

Thank you for purchasing Not My Daughter (Eva Rae Thomas #17). This story is inspired by a real story where a girl murdered her mom and blamed the whole thing on a good friend and classmate. I read it, and the story grew from there. You can read more here if you're interested:

https://www.oxygen.com/killer-couples/crime-time/lesbian-love-affair-between-teen-and-older-lover-ends-up-with-mother-stabbed

As usual, I want to thank you for all your support.
Please leave a review if you can.
Take care,

Willow

About the Author

Willow Rose is a multi-million-copy best-selling Author and an Amazon ALL-star Author of more than 100 novels.

Several of her books have reached the top 10 of ALL books in the Amazon store in the US, UK, and Canada.

She has sold more than six million books that are translated into many languages.

Willow's books are fast-paced, nail-biting pageturners with twists you won't see coming.

That's why her fans call her The Queen of Plot Twists.

Willow lives on Florida's Space Coast. When she is not writing or reading, you will find her surfing and watching the dolphins play in the waves of the Atlantic Ocean.

Join Willow Rose's VIP Newsletter to get exclusive updates about New Releases, Giveaways, and FREE ebooks.

Just scan this QR code with your phone and click on the link:

Cover design by Juan Villar Padron,
https://www.juanjpadron.com

Special thanks to my editor Janell Parque
http://janellparque.blogspot.com/